THE SHUTTERED WARD

JENNIFER ROSE MCMAHON

Copyright © 2019 by Jennifer Rose McMahon

All rights reserved.

No part of this book may be reproduced in any form or by any electronic or mechanical means, including information storage and retrieval systems, without written permission from the author, except for the use of brief quotations in a book review.

Cover design by Rebecca Frank

Edited by Cynthia Shepp

Dubhdara Publishing

PRAISE FOR JENNIFER ROSE MCMAHON

"McMahon's excellent paranormal mystery. Teen and adult readers alike will be clamoring for the sequel."

— PUBLISHERS WEEKLY STARRED REVIEW

"Engaging, beautifully written scenes, and idyllic descriptions keep the tale moving at a quick pace. The characters are engaging and they draw a person in to this tale of adventure and intrigue. Adrenaline-fueled action and enough twists and turns to keep even the most astute readers on their toes, this is a captivating story with a heroine who is forcefully engaging."

— IND'TALE MAGAZINE

"As Chieftain of The O'Malley Clan I am always interested in anything to do with Granuaile, our very famous Pirate Queen ancestor. Jennifer's novel captures the connection with the past which we treasure in Ireland. The Irish landscape, contemporary social life, the Irish language, and romance are woven into this fantasy story about Maeve Grace O'Malley and her quest to solve her 'Awake Dreams'. I am certainly looking forward to the sequel. More BOHERMORE please!"

— SARAH KELLY, O'MALLEY CLAN CHIEFTAIN 2017

To the souls who struggled with mental health conditions in a time when they were misunderstood. May they never be forgotten.

Remember us for we too have lived, loved and laughed.

— PLAQUE AT MEDFIELD STATE HOSPITAL

BOOK ONE ASYLUM SAVANTS SERIES

THE SHUTTERED WARD

by Jennifer Rose McMahon

CHAPTER 1

Whispers of echoing voices pulled me out of my bliss as an incessant beeping sound made my eyes twitch. But then the ferocious pounding struck, and I reached for my head to keep it from exploding.

My eyes shot open only to be blinded by the harsh illumination surrounding me. Shadows of unknown people hovered as one stepped closer and poked at my arm.

I squinted to block the piercing light, my voice scratching out of me. "Where's Kaitlin?"

A dark pit in my stomach swelled before rising into my throat. My memories wisped through my mind, murky as if lost in dense fog. When I tried to grab them, they slipped through my fingers. Everything seemed out of my reach except the heart-clenching need to check on Kaitlin. She was with me when…*when what?* I shook my head, only to be reminded of the painful, swollen pressure in my skull.

"She's okay, Grace," an unfamiliar voice said. The assurance rolled through my mind. "She's in the next room. Her parents are there, too."

With a slow exhale, I sank into the false comfort of my pillow and blocked out the activity around me. But in the sudden absence of stimulation, it hit me. The flash of headlights. A blaring horn. And a violent crash of bending metal and shattering glass that could have woken the dead.

We'd been in a car accident.

As we drove home from Braden's, we'd been struck from out of nowhere. And then everything had gone black.

Some memories—of a siren and flashing red lights—flickered, but I chose to ignore the chilling images.

"How long have I been here?" I mumbled through parched lips.

"Two days," the one who held my wrist, apparently checking for my pulse, replied. "We gave you something to help you rest. You took a big hit, dear. You're incredibly lucky."

Lucky? .

Go to hell.

I rolled to my side to escape the annoying stares, the nurse letting my arm go as I did.

I needed to know if Kaitlin was okay. As I squeezed my eyes shut, I pictured her in the room next to me. Similar shadows of hopeful people, watching for any sign of recovery. The same throbbing headache. Her angelic face, fighting the impact of the accident.

Then her eyes shot wide open. She stared into my soul, and I jolted in my bed with a gasp.

It was as if she'd seen me watching her.

My heartbeat accelerated through the roof. I sat straight up, causing everyone to jump. Throwing off my covers, I pulled at the tape and the tube that traveled along my arm, trying to free myself from the confines of the bed. Two firm hands pressed on my shoulders, pushing me down into the pillows.

"Grace, you need to rest." She nodded to another woman in scrubs. "We'll get you something to relax you now."

"No!" The word flew out of my mouth like a swear. With the fog in my head finally clearing, the last thing I wanted was more tranquilizing meds. Not to mention the feeling of being restrained was enough to make me violent. "No, please," I said with a calmer tone. "I'm okay. I don't need anything."

The shadow of a figure at the back stepped forward. "You need to do what they tell you, Grace. You're hurt."

My mother's voice grated on me like coarse sandpaper.

"I'm fine, Mom. Just a little banged up," I mumbled. "But I actually feel pretty good."

It was weird. My muscles screamed out in pain whenever I moved them. My head throbbed like my brain was trying to burst out of it. But still, I felt unusually…good.

I had a clarity I'd never felt before—even through the cotton-filled haze of my head injury. I knew what was right for me, and it didn't include meds or bed rest.

"I need to see Kaitlin," I said as I threw my legs over the edge of the bed.

The head rush nearly made me fall back into the pillows, but I steadied myself with my hands by my sides. The spinning in the room only lasted a minute, and I blinked into the blur of faces. My mother, two nurses, and a priest.

"What's he doing here?" I blurted out while glaring at my mother. She always went too far—raising the bar to get the most attention possible.

"Just to be safe," Mom said. "We didn't know how bad things might be."

Rolling my eyes, I turned my head away from them. I always hated her reliance on the church when it came to anything to do with me. I didn't believe in it, and his presence alone sent sickening annoyance through my veins. Plus, the whole religion thing was just Mom's excuse for never connecting with me. She was always too involved with their services or the choir. It was her own form of addiction, like an alcoholic or a pill-popper, to avoid real life. Only her choice of drug was more socially acceptable.

Her unwavering loyalty to an arguably dying institution left me feeling confused and insecure. Being her only child, yet unimportant in comparison, created a deep scar that ached with the despair of being lost.

That was it.

I was lost.

Alone.

My dad had left us when I was a baby. I tried not to feel bad about it. I'd been too young for him to know me, so I tried to convince myself it wasn't my fault. I never knew why he left, but Mom said it was mental illness. It was probably the easiest explanation for her to latch on to. And so I believed it.

Seeing Mom next to her priest made me begin to question the truth in her lies, though. There was mental illness, all right, but maybe it wasn't in my dad.

"Please." I turned to the nurse as I tugged on the tape. "Help me out of this." The nurse glanced to my mother for approval, making my blood boil. "Umm, no. I'm nineteen years old. I don't need my mother's permission to get out of bed." I glared at her until she made a move to assist me.

"You might be unsteady on your feet," the nurse said as she tugged at the tape, ripping out my arm hairs in the process. I eyed the IV port, noticing blood had backed up into the line. My stomach turned, causing my head to spin. "Easy. Just take a minute to get your balance." She reached under my shoulder as the other nurse brought a walker over to the bed.

I pressed up to standing, immediately feeling the weakness in my muscles after two days of not moving, but I was determined to walk out of that room—on my own.

Stepping forward in baby steps, I moved past the walker, refusing its assistance. With each additional step, the nurse's grasp under my shoulder lightened.

"Thanks," I said. "I got this." I stepped out of my room. With a hand at the wall, I moved down the hallway toward the next door.

As I got closer, I heard the soft mumbling of voices, but then, like an unexpected siren, a scream shot terror through me. The scream turned to sickening moans and wails, causing my heart to nearly pound out of my chest.

My pace tripled as my shuffling steps turned to wide gaits, and I threw myself toward her open door.

Standing in the doorway, I stared in disbelief as they restrained Kaitlin's flailing body. Her screams pierced through my skull as she called for me.

"Grace," she screeched. "Don't let them take me there!"

Kaitlin's screams shot terror through me, and I pushed past the nurses in her room to get to her bed. As soon as her eyes fell on me, she stopped yelling and thrashing. She stared at me with a confused expression in her eye, then she scanned the others in the room. Her head dropped, and she gazed at her sheets.

I pressed in closer to her bed, then grabbed on to her hand. "Kaitlin, you're okay," I said. "I am, too."

Her eyes lifted to mine. She gave a weak smile, exposing her teeth. "I feel dumb," she mumbled, glancing at the staff. "I don't know why I freaked out like that. Sorry." Her gaze fell again.

Squeezing her hand, I said, "Don't worry, Kaitlin. We were in an accident. But we're okay."

She nodded. "Yeah. I guess so."

One of her nurses pulled a heavy armchair over to me. The blue vinyl upholstery squeaked when I sat on it, and I inched it closer to the top of Kaitlin's bed.

"We'll leave you two to chat for a bit," one of the nurses said. "Press this button if you need assistance." She placed a controller with a red button onto Kaitlin's lap.

In silence, we watched the nurses leave the room. One looked back with a curious glance, then moved down the hall out of sight.

I hopped up, then closed the door as quietly as possible.

"Holy shit, Kaitlin," I blurted as I fell onto my chair. "What the hell happened to us?" I rubbed the side of my skull that throbbed the most.

"I don't know. It all happened so fast." Her hands lifting, she gripped around her face. "My head feels like it's stuffed with cotton. And like its hollow at the same time."

"I think we have concussions," I grumbled. "Makes sense, anyway." I looked into her face, studying it. "Why were you screaming like that? You scared the shit out of me."

She moved the controller off her legs. It fell along the side of the bed, swinging from its cord. "I'm not sure." She bit her lip. "It was like we were torn away from each other. I thought you were gone." She swallowed hard. "And then the way the nurses looked at me like they thought I was crazy. It was like one of those creepy movies where they take you to a padded room and throw away the key."

I nodded. "Yeah. I kinda felt that, too, in *my* room." I exhaled through my nose, replaying the unsettling glances from the nurses in my mind. "Like they were studying me. Trying to figure out if I was normal or not, I guess."

"I don't know," Kaitlin said. "It just felt like they held too much power. Like they could actually hurt me." She stared at me with worry in her gaze. "It was terrifying, actually."

"I think the best thing we can do right now is convince them we're fine and ready to go home." I continued, planning out loud. "Once we're out of here, we can at least be in control again. I just don't like the way they look at us in here. Like they're in charge of us or something." Glancing at the door, I listened for any sign of footsteps. "So, anytime they ask, just say you're feeling much better. Eat all your food and walk around and shit. There's no way they can keep us here if we seem fine."

Kaitlin pushed herself up higher in her bed. "Help me get out of this before my parents come back."

After I pulled the covers off her, she shimmied to the edge of the bed. She planted her sock-covered feet on the tile floor before looking up at me. We held each other's gaze for a moment. In that brief eye lock, a chill of death coursed through my veins as I saw us running for our lives, screaming. With a loud gasp, I ripped my gaze away.

Kaitlin's hand flew to her mouth. "What, Grace? Did you see that, too?" she whispered.

It was a memory I had no recollection of. But it was so vivid.

"We were running," I murmured.

Her eyes widened like she'd seen a ghost as her harrowed gaze searched mine. She swallowed hard and said, "Yes. Running for our lives."

CHAPTER 2

Being held like a prisoner against my will made me want to tear my hair out. Everyone around me was an enemy until the moment of discharge. Being released from the hospital was the most liberating feeling I'd ever had, though it made no sense.

The medical staff was only trying to help me get well. Nothing sinister was going on. But deep in my soul, I was trapped. And I had to get out.

They said my paranoia was part of my healing—everyone responded to a concussion differently. I'd seen athletes at my high school with concussions, and they seemed fine. They acted like nothing was wrong. But right before my release, the nurses at the hospital kept calling my condition a traumatic brain injury. That term made it sound so much worse.

Kaitlin, too. She had the same diagnosis.

They told us to expect fatigue and brain fog for a while. But they'd also said our 'young brains' would heal quickly. New neurological connections would be made. And, in the end, we'd be fine. However, they also warned us about emotional outbursts, depression, anxiety, and slow processing for some time. It was the slow processing that bothered me the most. I was used to being a quick thinker and an astute problem solver.

Then, my mind jumped to the cause of my injury.

I wanted to see the car.

I wasn't sure why but replaying the actual scene of the accident and seeing what happened became my primary focus. And then my obsession.

I grabbed my phone to Facetime Kaitlin, called, and waited as the ringing continued. Propping the pillows on my bed, I sat up straight and gathered my thick brown hair, twisting it into a messy bun at the top of my head.

When she finally picked up, I asked, "How's your head? Feeling dumb?"

Kaitlin rubbed her temple where her bruising was. It had drained into her right eye, making it look like she'd been beaten. The deep color of her mahogany brown eyes made it look even worse. She pulled her hair out from behind her ear, then used it to try to cover the purple-and-yellow shadows. Her blunt cut worked against her, though, and the hair fell uncooperatively along the side of her face.

"All right, I guess." She smirked. "Still headachy, but the fog is gone. I'm actually thinking clearly right now."

I blinked and scanned my own condition, turning my attention into my mind. She was right. I had clarity as well, and I actually felt sharp.

"This might sound weird, but I want to see what happened," I said. "Like, where it happened. And the condition of the car. I don't know why. It's just bugging me."

"Me too," she blasted into my screen. "It's all I've been thinking about!"

I huffed out a puff of air, then smiled. "Should I text Braden? He could take us."

"Ya, do it," she said. Then she pushed her face right into her phone, filling my entire screen with her nose. "And tell him to bring Nick."

I typed into my phone.

"Did you do it?" Kaitlin asked.

"Yup. I'll let you know when he responds."

Two seconds later, I checked to see if he'd opened it, but disappointment from the unopened symbol poked at me, no matter how irrational.

"I can't believe the hospital wouldn't allow any visitors," Kaitlin added. "They made it feel like a prison."

I narrowed my eyes. "I bet my mother had something to do with it. She always tries to make it difficult for me to hang out with friends. Even you. It's annoying."

"It's like she thinks I'm bad for you or something," Kaitlin said. "I always get the feeling she doesn't like me."

"And that's so stupid," I blurted. "You're my best friend. Doesn't she know she's only pushing me closer to you when she acts like that?" I shook my head. "She thinks all her rules and restrictions will make me want to stay home and like, read the bible or something."

Kaitlin chuckled. "Did Braden open it yet?"

I checked my messages.

"Shit! Yes!" I scanned his response. "He said yes with a bunch of Ss. And asked when."

"Tell him today," Kaitlin urged.

She was just as eager as I was to explore the details of the night of the accident. I didn't understand why, but it was all either of us could think about now.

After I typed back, his reply came quickly.

"He said okay," I told Kaitlin. "And then he asked if we were sure."

Hesitating, I watched her through my phone. She paused as well, then said, "I'm sure."

I wondered why he had asked that. It was almost like a warning. Like maybe it was a bad idea.

Shrugging off the odd feeling, I responded, "Yeah, I'm sure, too," to Kaitlin.

I stalked Kaitlin on my phone, watching her cruising along my Snap map in a little red car. She'd be here any minute. Minus the cute little red car. Instead, she'd be a passenger in her mom's SUV since we weren't allowed to drive yet. They said our response time might be delayed or we'd be easily distracted while our brains healed. It was over-kill, but her parents and my mom played by the book so there was no getting around that one.

It had been five days since the accident, and I was more than ready to get on with my summer. It was the first vacation in years I didn't have the pressure of constant soccer practices or boring reading assignments that nagged the entire time. I was free. Until September, of course, when I'd head off to college.

But I didn't want to think about that right now. It made my head hurt. Instead, I would do as my doctor ordered—rest and relax...with a little added adventure. I looked at my phone. We still had an hour before Braden and Nick would be here, and I bounced on the edge of my bed. The slamming of a door jolted my eyes to the window, and footsteps thumped across the wooden planks of my porch.

"My mom nearly didn't let me come," Kaitlin announced as she burst into the house. "She thinks 'rest' means full isolation and removal from society." She stumbled toward the couch with her hair strewn in every direction.

Her disheveled condition and high anxiety were typical, though, so I was relieved to see her acting like herself. It wasn't uncommon for her to fly into my house with bags of supplies to build a project due the next morning or to send panicked pics at eight in the morning, having just woken up, right when school was already starting. She was an emotional wreck most of the time, but I loved her that way.

"My mom's the same," I said. "I bet they talked and planned out how they would quarantine us. But screw that." I grabbed my phone, then updated my settings. "Ghost-mode."

Grinning, Kaitlin did the same. Now they couldn't track us.

A shudder ran through me, and my entire body twitched. The relief of not being confined quaked out of me, and I shook the final remnants out through my fingertips.

"God, I hate how controlling they are," I said. "Let's just do whatever this summer. I'm done reporting every move to my warden."

"Exactly." Kaitlin ran her hands through her hair to fix it. "I feel the same way. Time to break free!"

I smiled as this new feeling of rebellion coursed through me. It was a good feeling, like I'd suddenly grown up or was somehow wiser. Kaitlin's eyes held the same knowledge. It was an enlightenment.

"What happened to us?" I whispered. "It's like the accident finally knocked some sense into us."

Kaitlin's hand went to her mouth, and she bit her thumbnail. "I don't know. But I've honestly never been clearer in my head than I am now. It's like we were brainwashed minions all this time. And now we're just…us."

"I hope it stays this way," I said. "Like, I hope once we're all better, we don't go back to normal. I don't want this feeling to go away."

"Let's just make sure it doesn't then," Kaitlin said. "We need to keep reminding each other of this moment. And to keep moving forward with it."

"Deal." An ache pounded behind my left eye, and I squinted. "They're gonna be here soon." I peeked out the window.

"Shit," Kaitlin burst out. "I look like shit." She ran to my room, then dropped into my vanity chair. Leaning into the mirror, she poked at her cheeks and her eyes. "I'm a mess."

"You're gorgeous, Kaitlin," I said. Her natural features made up for any lack of sleep or brain trauma. Besides, she had a perfect complexion and had always worn little or no makeup.

"Whatever," she mumbled. "It's a lost cause next to you, anyway. How do you always look so good?" She pushed at her bottom lip as she continued to stare into the mirror. "Your eyelashes and those blue eyes… it's just unfair. Braden's not the only one who follows you around like a lost puppy."

"That's so untrue," I said, glancing at my phone. "I've never even had a real boyfriend."

"Okay, whatever." Kaitlin rolled her eyes, and our phones vibrated at the same time. "They're here!"

She jumped off the chair, nearly knocking it to the ground, and ran down the hall in a frenzy. I followed her, wondering why I felt so unusually calm. My heart hadn't changed pace in the least, while her actions seemed to say hers had quadrupled its rate.

We stepped onto the porch, and I turned to lock the door. My mother wouldn't be home from work for hours, and the freedom that lay ahead of me was exhilarating.

"I feel free," I said.

A smile moved across Kaitlin's face. "Yeah. Me too."

I stared down the walkway at Braden's idling car, a knot forming in my stomach. "But why does it feel strange to go with them?" I stood frozen in my spot.

Kaitlin glanced at the car and then back to me. "It doesn't," she said, reaching for my arm. "Come on!"

She pulled me off the porch and we bounced down the walkway, each step twisting my gut a little more.

It was like entering unfamiliar territory. I had no idea why. I'd been in Braden's car a million times.

But something was different today. Like we were embarking on a new quest.

And it felt unnerving.

∼

The guys turned around and stared at us in the backseat like they were looking at the walking dead. It was as if they were checking to see if we were any different. And somehow, we were.

"I thought you'd be more banged up," Braden said.

"Yeah, like with big bandages wrapped around your heads like turbans or something," Nick added.

Braden punched him in the arm, then looked at me.

"No, seriously, are you okay?" he asked, searching my eyes.

I nodded. "Yeah, surprisingly. I think I'm okay. Kaitlin, too." I glanced to her for assurance.

"Yeah," Kaitlin said. "But maybe it's the calm before the storm," she mumbled.

"What does that mean?" Braden asked

Kaitlin shrugged. "I don't know. They say it could get worse before it gets better."

She glanced at me worriedly. Like she had no idea what to expect.

"We're fine," I added in a curt tone. I had no time for Kaitlin's anxiety at the moment. Particularly if it had anything to do with me not healing right. I didn't need to add that to my list of worries.

"Looks like you got punched in the eye," Nick said, gesturing at Kaitlin.

Reaching up, she rubbed the yellowing bruise under her eye. "Thanks."

Braden put the car in drive and pulled out, causing Nick to face forward as well.

I glanced at Kaitlin with pursed lips. Nick was a dick, and she knew what I thought about him.

Kaitlin lifted her shoulders, batting her lashes at me. She knew he was a dick, too. But she also thought he was hot, and his hotness trumped all in her mind.

"Do you know where my car is?" I asked Braden.

"Yeah. I've driven by it a million times," he said. "It's at Central Garage. I wish they'd get rid of it."

I knew the lot he meant. Some of their cars there were mangled, while others were only fender benders.

"Is it bad?" I asked.

"No, not really," he said. "But the airbags went off, so it's probably a total loss."

I pushed my bottom lip out. There went my travel freedom. It was Mom's hand-me-down when she downsized to a small two-door. But now it would be near impossible to get a replacement.

"Well, I just need to see it," I added. "Like a kind of farewell, I guess."

Braden turned onto Central Street. The familiar green road sign pointed east for Boston and west for Worcester. We were trapped somewhere in between—west suburban abyss.

"It looks like they've moved it to the back," he said. "It was in the front row for days, taunting me." He pulled into the lot. "There it is." He rolled through the lines of cars, some crashed, others with 'for sale' signs on them.

My stomach twisted into a knot, and I pressed my hand to it. I lifted my gaze to Kaitlin, catching her doing the exact same thing.

Braden stopped the car. "That's it."

I held Kaitlin's eyes, refusing to look out at my car. She struggled to hold my gaze, like she didn't want to see it either.

"We have to, Kaitlin," I said. "Come on." I reached for my door handle and pulled on it.

We climbed out of the car, keeping our eyes down, and waited for the guys. Nick hopped out, fidgeting as Braden came around to us.

"So, you gonna look at it?" Nick asked.

"Give them a second, asshole," Braden interjected. "This is serious."

I huffed, appreciating Braden's support while confirming my original judgment of Nick's character. I seriously didn't know what Kaitlin saw in him. And I wasn't even sure why Braden hung out with him.

"Ready?" I asked Kaitlin.

"Yup."

I turned toward the car, then took a step forward. As I raised my gaze to it, the image of the vehicle flooded all my senses, erupting a surge of emotion. Like a flashing slideshow, a series of pictures blasted through my mind. Driving and laughing with Kaitlin. Bright lights and a blaring horn. Crashing metal and exploding airbags. Numbers. An array of repeating numbers. A license plate, maybe? A road sign? 235236. I shook my head to clear the haunting images.

"Are you okay?" Braden's voice echoed in the back of my mind.

I turned to Kaitlin as if in slow motion, seeing her face frozen in a silent scream. She reached for her head, ducking it down as she hunched over.

"Kaitlin," I shouted. "What's wrong!" She crunched down as if straining against the memories of the accident. I reached for her. "It's okay, Kaitlin. I feel it, too It's overwhelming."

She mumbled incoherently as she squeezed her head harder.

I looked at the car. The front end was crushed. I'd been told the driver of the other car fell asleep and went through a stop sign. He had no idea of the damage he had truly caused us. Traumatic brain injury. And psychological trauma. PTSD—they'd warned us of its sinister effect.

I turned to Braden. His nervous eyes studied me as if he questioned his decision to bring us here. Leaning into Kaitlin, I held her trembling shoulders. Her mumbles grew louder, and I strained to hear.

"235236," she whispered, over and over.

CHAPTER 3

The repeating numbers fell from her mouth, mixing with the ones in my own head, like a spell or a chant. I was sure she would conjure a demon if she didn't stop the incessant rant. But the worst part was they were the same numbers that had flashed through *my* mind. We'd seen the same thing. And now, with the help of the torturous flashbacks of PTSD, they repeated through our minds, over and over.

"It's okay, Kaitlin," I tried to soothe her. "I saw the same numbers. I've no clue what they are." I glanced up at Braden, watching him shift his weight from one foot to the other. "Let's get out of here."

Within seconds, we were back in his car bombing down Central. Kaitlin rocked in her seat while I fought vile cramps in my stomach.

"Maybe that wasn't such a good idea," Braden said, studying me in the rearview mirror.

I shook my head at him. "No. It's okay. We had to do it."

I glanced at Kaitlin again. It was clear she hadn't been ready for it, though. Her mind had blown more than mine, and the pieces were still scattered all over the place.

Taking a deep breath, I put my window down. "Let's just drive. Like, through those country roads down 27. By the orchards."

Kaitlin perked up as if her head had suddenly cleared. Inhaling deeply, she sat taller.

"Yeah. Let's try to find that lost cemetery again," she mumbled. "Anything to change the subject, basically."

She had shifted back to our urban-explorer's mindset. That was a good sign, like she was returning to herself again.

We'd searched that area before, looking for an old, forgotten cemetery. Kaitlin and I loved hunting for mysteries that held secrets just out of our reach. We always kept an eye out for anything supernatural or haunted. Old cemeteries were the best.

"You guys are so weird," Nick snarled. "Cemeteries are lame. They're just full of dead people."

"It's not that," I said. "They're actually peaceful. And full of stories and history." I tried to articulate why I loved old graveyards so much. They fascinated me, holding secrets of the past in their silent realm.

"People say they hear screaming at night, coming from the area," Braden added in a sinister tone. "It has a violent history, they say. Like, psycho-killers are buried there."

"Shit," Nick said. "Now it's sounding interesting."

Braden swerved along the winding roads, and we moved farther from our highly populated residential area to the more woodsy roads of Sherborn and Medfield. We referred to the back roads of those towns as 'out the country'.

"There's the water tower," Kaitlin pointed.

Over the treetops, the bulbous blue tank of the area's water supply hovered on long legs above the tree line, like an alien robot coming to annihilate us.

"That thing's so creepy," I said. "How does it even work?" I shuddered from the sight of it. It was the same feeling I got when I would swim near a buoy and my foot touched the chain that secured it to the bottom of the dark depths. Full-on heebie-jeebies.

"The cemetery's supposed to be somewhere near the water tower," Kaitlin said to Braden. "Just follow the road in that direction."

I smirked at Kaitlin. It was weird how much we enjoyed this kind of adventure, but it was exactly what we needed at the moment. A full distraction from the accident as well as the weirdness we felt in our heads. And the numbers. The repeating numbers. I couldn't clear them from my mind, and they picked at my brain like a curious probe.

Braden turned down a narrow lane that seemed to move in the direction of the tower. The tree cover blocked our view, so we relied on our sense of direction at that point.

"Is this someone's driveway?" Nick asked. "Wouldn't want to shovel this shit in the winter."

The road narrowed, and Braden slowed the car. "Look at that..." He pointed to the sides. "It's like an old gateway of some sort."

Pushing to the edge of my seat, I leaned out the window. On my side of the road was a stone structure covered in ivy and moss. Directly across from it was an identical structure, like they were connected at one time. Rusted nubs protruded from the sides, and I figured metal gates used to be there to block entry.

"Do you think this could be it?" Braden asked. His voice stuck in his throat with each passing syllable.

"I'm not sure." I shimmied to the center of the backseat, gazing out the windshield. "I don't remember hearing that it was so isolated. Like so deep in the woods."

"Yeah, me neither," Kaitlin agreed. "This seems more like a private drive to an estate or something."

"Should we go back?" Braden asked.

"Hell no," Nick interjected. "It's just starting to get interesting."

A shiver ran through me, sending warning to my gut. Kaitlin's wide eyes proved she'd felt the same jitters.

Bending closer to her, I whispered, "Have we been here before?"

She gasped, body tense. "I was just wondering the same thing."

We had been warned that unusual flashbacks would be a part of our brain recovery, but this eerie, familiar feeling was more like deja vu. And nausea. Combined.

"What? Do you recognize this place or something?" Braden asked.

I stared at Kaitlin, waiting for the answer that already nagged at the back of my brain.

"No, I don't think so," I said. "It's just...it's like it's from a movie we saw or something. Sort of familiar."

"And there's a feeling," Kaitlin added with a quake in her shoulders.

"Let's hope it wasn't a horror movie," Nick joked. "Particularly the kind with chainsaws and shit."

I huffed and then asked Braden, "Should we walk a bit? You could pull over on the grass there." I pointed ahead, just past one of the stone structures.

"Yeah, sure," he replied. "I don't think the car would make it much farther anyway. The road gets pretty narrow up ahead, it looks overgrown."

We climbed out of the car after Braden parked it, then began walking along the dirt passage. Two lone tire marks cut up along the lane, proving the road got little use.

The brightness of day became shrouded by the heavy evergreen boughs above, and shadows grew darker with the thickness of the overgrowth. Midday felt more like a foggy evening in the dense canopy.

Our footsteps crunched in the loose gravel while the four of us scanned the woods on either side, searching for clues of a hidden cemetery.

"Where the hell is the fog coming from?" Nick asked. "Did the director cue the fog machine? I mean, it's summer. And daytime."

Surveying the conditions of the forest, I calculated the moisture in the air. "It's just condensed water droplets. A result of the air being cooled to dew point so it can no longer hold the water vapor in suspension. Rising air, that's cooled from expansion, is likely the cause." I stopped when I noticed everyone staring at me. "You know, the forest floor is cool. Soil doesn't hold heat." My voice trailed off.

"Um, I thought you bombed bio?" Kaitlin teased.

Numeric calculations coursed through my mind, showing me the probability and statistics of things I didn't give a crap about.

"Yeah, I guess I retained more than I realized," I mumbled. "All of it, actually." I squeezed my eyes shut to clear my mind of the running list of calculations and analytical information. It felt like a computer was processing through my brain, and I understood every pulse and code.

I opened my eyes again only to find everyone still staring at me.

Something about this place had tapped into my memories. My subconscious. It awakened knowledge I had stored away in tidy, secret compartments. And now all those sealed doors within my brain had opened at once. The rush was exhilarating. But at the same time, it was embarrassing.

"Come on," I said. "Never mind my weather forecasting. I'm a bit of a closet science geek," I lied. "So now you know."

I started walking again, and they followed along.

Within two seconds, Kaitlin caught up. "What the hell was that?"

"What?" I peeked at her from the corner of my eyes.

"Information," she said. "Is your mind exploding with mundane, trivial facts?"

I stopped in my tracks. Her bottom lip quivered.

"Kaitlin?" I said. "Is it happening to you, too?"

Her eyes shot to the guys to make sure they weren't listening. "Yes. Grace, I'm scared. What is this place?"

"It's not the place, Kaitlin," I assured her. "It's our brains. They're rewiring. Remember?" I rubbed my temple absentmindedly. "The doctors told us our neural connections had been damaged. And now they need to find new pathways. So, it's just tapping into shit that's already in our heads, I think. Makes sense, right?"

"I guess," she whispered. "I mean, we suffered the same impact. So, makes sense our recovery would be similar." She held her head for a moment. "But I feel like I can't control it. My mind is expanding, like beyond my skull."

"Okay, that sounds more like a migraine, Kaitlin," I said. "That's one of our symptoms, too, so let's not blow this out of proportion." I watched her clench her jaw. "Do you want to get out of here?"

"No, I want to find the freakin' cemetery," she blasted. "I'm not leaving until we do."

I laughed at her persistence. A true urban explorer.

Fatigue already weighed down my muscles, though, and I wasn't sure how long we'd last. "Let's go a little farther. Just to see if anything looks interesting."

Braden and Nick had wandered ahead while Kaitlin and I chatted, so we ran to catch up to them.

"Hey, there's something up ahead," Braden called to us.

Our feet scurried along the uneven, broken pavement as we caught up.

Just off to the side of the road was a large sign. Vines grew over it, making it difficult to read. Braden stepped into the weeds and pulled at them, exposing the white sign, attached to a broad, solid stone monument. The fancy black lettering read:

Blackwood State Hospital

"I heard that place was shut down," Nick said. "Like a ghost town."

He was right. I remembered hearing urban legends about the hospital, too, like all the buildings were boarded up and falling apart. And some said it was haunted by former patients. I hadn't thought it still existed, though. I thought they tore it down years ago.

"Wanna check it out?" Braden turned to me.

I swallowed hard, side-eying at Kaitlin. She nodded.

"Sure," I said, glancing back to Braden.

I stepped near the sign, then ran my hand along the top of it. White paint chipped along the wooden edge, and the black, fading letters held their own secrets within the eerie script. As I moved closer, my foot caught in one of the creeping vines, making me stumble. I grabbed onto the edge of the worn sign. My fingers gripped the wooden plaque to steady myself, but it broke away from the stone monument that held it.

"Shit!" I gasped, fearing I'd vandalized the relic.

The sign wobbled on loosened screws that had eroded from the granite over time. The corner of the wooden plaque I'd grabbed on to had separated from the landmark, exposing etched letters carved into the stone behind it. My eyes widened with curiosity, and I pulled at the corner of the broken sign to expose what it so cautiously hid within the granite.

"What are you doing?" Kaitlin jumped forward. "Don't make it worse."

"I'm not," I muttered through my intense focus. "There's something here."

I pulled the wooden sign farther from the granite monument, exposing more stone-carved lettering. The gothic script filled my vision as the entire board pulled away and dropped to the ground, exposing the original, hidden sign.

My hand flew to my mouth as I gasped and backed away.

"Fuck." Nick stepped back, eyes wildly darting around.

Braden stood frozen, staring at the exposed, original marker.

Kaitlin moved to my side as we read the authentic sign together. Over and over.

Blackwood Insane Asylum
Est. 1896

It started in my hands, traveled up my arms, then shot through my entire body. The frightful trembling turned to spastic shudders as fear coursed through me like a toxic venom.

"That's freaky," I choked, stepping through the vines to get away from the sign.

The words 'insane asylum' held a sick amount of power and judgment that turned my stomach. Poor souls from the not-so-distant past were sent there, most likely against their wills. Then the politicians probably thought a name change from asylum to hospital would improve the image of the institution. I looked back at the permanency of the stone marker and then at the broken, rotted attempt at hiding the truth—the wooden sign that now lay on the ground in its failure.

"So...," Braden glanced in the direction of the road that led to the asylum. "Shall we?"

I noticed Kaitlin's blanched complexion, white as a ghost. "Are you okay?" I asked. She looked like she was about to puke.

"Just lightheaded," she said as she dropped her hands to her knees. "I'm gonna need to lie down soon."

She was right. I felt it, too We were supposed to be resting, to recover our brains. And my body screamed to slow down, turn off the lights, and do nothing.

But there was no way we could stop now. This discovery was way too exciting. It was everything Kaitlin and I had always searched for.

I turned to Braden. He watched me with raised eyebrows.

"Are you sure you're up for this?" he asked. "You should probably be resting or something. We're not exactly prepared for a full-scale adventure."

He knew me too well. Knew I'd never back away from such a discovery. Always enticed by signs that said, 'do not enter' or 'stay off the grass'. I saw them more as a challenge than a demand or request.

The pulse in my temples grew stronger, and I realized my headache meds were wearing off. I had no water and basically nothing to help the situation. But still, there was no way I was turning back now. We at least had to see what was up ahead.

"Let's check it out and then decide what to do," I said. "I can't not know what's up there."

Kaitlin stumbled out of the brush, then back onto the road next to me. "My curiosity is killing me," she said as she reached for my arm and locked her elbow with mine.

Nick walked ahead while Braden stayed closer, keeping a close eye on me. He was always nervous about following rules and doing what was right. It was cute. Most of the time. But right now, I could tell it was going to enter the smothering zone at any moment. I had to assure him we were fine.

"I think being out in the fresh air and getting some exercise is probably good for us." Smiling, I started walking in the direction of the asylum. Kaitlin dragged at first but then kept up.

"Okay," he said. "If you're sure."

Braden's long strides moved him along the road faster than us, and he started to catch up to Nick. Braden's tall frame shadowed Nick, making his short stature even more prominent. No wonder Nick always had to act big in his comments and actions. It was his Napoleon complex. And he never disappointed.

"Concussions are for pussies, anyway," Nick yelled back to us. "You guys are fine."

I shook my head, glaring at Kaitlin.

She squeezed my elbow with hers. "Yeah, but he's hot." And she keeled over, giggling.

"Oh my God." I splatted my hand on my forehead.

"Have you seen those eyes?" she continued. "I can barely look at them when I talk to him."

I chuckled, knowing she was trapped by his primal features. I supposed I couldn't blame her. She was right about his eyes.

I turned my attention to Braden. I'd always liked him, but I'd never made a move on him. I wasn't sure how I felt, like if it was brotherly love or if I was attracted to him. I wished I could decide, especially for his sake.

He was very patient, but it was obvious he was waiting for me. And I couldn't find any flaws, which made my indecision even worse. He was tall and good looking. Athletic and kind. He was smart and funny. I watched him like I always did, trying to picture myself with him. But then, as usual, right when I'm about to accept it, the feelings become confused and leave me uncertain, unknowing.

Then Nick's voice blasted me out of my inner thoughts and back to the moment. His voice sent shock waves through my body that jolted me to attention.

"There's something up ahead," he yelled. "A clearing. And I see a brick building all boarded up!"

CHAPTER 4

We raced toward the clearing to see the ominous boarded-up building. My mind swam with intrigue as I pictured an old insane asylum in full operation—patients chained to beds, padded rooms, screaming to be let out.

Clearly, I'd seen too many movies and prayed this place hadn't ever been like that. But then, I considered the antiquated practices in mental health of the past century. It involved lobotomies, shock therapy, and solitary confinement. Misunderstood mental illness was seen as demonic possession or stubborn defiance. Now, those conditions would be called something like bi-polar or manic depression and instead of horrific torture treatments, there would be proper therapies and medications.

A chill ran through me as I thought about the poor souls who'd been trapped in there. Now boarded up forever.

"Check this out," Nick shouted, waving for us to hurry up.

Kaitlin and I pulled our eyes from the brick building, following Nick's gaze. He stared at a small sign hanging from a wooden post at the entrance to the grounds. Its words slowed my breathing as if the spirits were speaking directly to me.

Remember us for we, too, have lived, loved, and laughed.

The blue lettering was framed by a set of angel wings and a swirling scroll at the bottom.

It was meant to be some kind of memorial of remembrance. Instead, I read it as more of a warning. A reminder that souls were lost. Mistreated. And only now recognized as fellow humans.

Tears stung at my eyes, and my throat tightened. It felt like we were treading on sacred ground, seeing something that should remain unseen.

"Come on," Nick called. "What are you waiting for?"

My attention moved from the sign to him. I hadn't noticed he and Braden had moved farther into the grounds while Kaitlin and I hovered at the perimeter.

"I feel sick," Kaitlin said.

My stomach clamped on itself, sending nausea through me as well.

"Me too. Let's not stay too long," I said. "I just want to have a quick look around. We can always come back another time."

She nodded, and we hurried to catch up to the guys.

As we got closer to the boarded-up brick building, the space expanded in front of us, bringing dozens of buildings into our view. The area was immense, like a small town or traditional college campus. An old paved road connected the numerous buildings, and a clock tower rose from what looked like a chapel in the center of the grounds. The face of the clock was faded and chipped, with several missing Roman numerals and no hands left. Still though, it stood proud as a sentinel over the institution and held tight to its many secrets.

"Holy crap," Braden exclaimed. "This place is huge."

Each building held its own unique character and architectural structure. The chapel was the most obvious with its oversized, arched doorway and tall, narrow stained-glass windows running along the side. Some other buildings resembling college dorms and maybe even a library. There was a loading dock that ran along the side of one of the simpler structures. But every building had the same red brick construction with slate roofing along all the peaks, and every single window at ground level was boarded up with secure plywood coverings.

"It's like a prison," Nick murmured, looking around with a trepidatious frown.

"I don't know," I said. "At the time, I bet this gothic architecture was considered beautiful."

"I kinda get the prison-vibe, too," Braden added. "I wouldn't want to be trapped here. This place is spooky."

We walked along the road and moved farther into the grounds. The silence around us added to the ethereal feel of the abandoned space. Wind moved through the trees, causing the leaves to rustle, bringing a breath of life to the stillness of the area.

I stopped, gazing at a large walnut tree in the center green across from the chapel. Its heavy branches were thick and reached in every direction around it. It had to be hundreds of years old, judging by the width of the trunk.

One branch in particular caught my attention. It reached out from the side of the tree horizontally, holding the weight of smaller branches and leaves at the end of it. The section that shot out from the trunk was clean, without offshoots. I stared at it until my eyes faded out of focus.

Then, an image flashed in my mind. A rope hung from the branch. Twisting from the bottom of it was a young woman. Hanging by the neck.

I gasped, then a small shriek escaped my lips.

"What the fuck is that?" Kaitlin cried, grabbing on to my arm again. She pulled at me, yanking me back. "Let's get the hell out of here," she yelled to the guys. "Oh my God, Grace!" She leaned over, retching from what she had also seen—the horrific sight of the dead girl hanging from the tree. "Get me out of here."

I retreated as the woman's swollen, purple face filled my mind with terror. Her dead eyes held mine in a final call for help.

"Let's go," I shouted at Braden and Nick as they hurried toward us with puzzled expressions.

"What's up?" Braden called. "You okay?" His worried tone confused me.

And then, I realized something that made my stomach drop. He hadn't seen her.

As he and Nick approached us, I turned toward the massive walnut tree and lifted my shaking finger, pointing toward the sinister branch.

"There," I said, peeking toward the horrific scene through one squinted eye.

But she was gone.

The branch held no evidence of her being there. No rope. No asphyxiation. I gaped at Braden in disbelief.

"There was a…a woman," I started. But just as the words left my mouth, I froze. There was movement just beyond where I had seen her hanging.

I stared beyond the walnut, toward the long building with the loading dock. And there, just beyond the line of vision where the woman hung, was a dark figure coming toward us.

∼

The vision of the woman hanging by her neck had rattled me to a point I couldn't think straight. Convincing myself it was my imagination was impossible because, unfortunately, Kaitlin's reaction to the horrific sight made it clear she had seen it, too. But before I had a chance to process it, I'd been jolted into fight-or-flight mode from the dark figure now headed toward us. And flight was my clear option of choice.

"Braden," I called, my voice squeaking out of me.

He was by my side instantly, keeping his eyes on the stranger, but glancing at me every few seconds. He had no idea what I had just seen, but he could tell something had shaken me.

As the stranger got closer, he slowed his pace and approached us with bright eyes and a warm smile. His graying hair and small-framed glasses paired with his brown tweed jacket gave him the appearance of a college professor or an administrator of some sort. But he appeared harmless enough.

"Hey there," he said. "So you guys found it."

His friendly face and relaxed stance put me at ease, but it was still unusual to have a stranger approach us in such a creepy place. I ducked behind Braden.

"Hey," Braden replied, his eyes narrowing. "Just looking around." He pushed me farther behind him, as if by instinct.

"Well, feel free. Looking is fine." He paused. "I'm the groundskeeper here, for the historical preservation committee," he added. "Sometimes, kids try to break into the buildings and whatnot, you understand." He glanced at each one of us. "Are you all familiar with the place?"

"No, first time," Braden said. "We actually just stumbled upon it."

"We've heard stories, though," Nick interjected. "I just didn't know if they were real or not."

"Oh, yeah." The man nodded. "It's real, all right. I know almost everything about its history, but something still seems to surprise me every time I'm here."

My spine straightened as I watched the man. He seemed good-natured, but I couldn't help being suspicious of him.

"How did you get here?" I asked with a judging tone and pinched eyes.

Everyone gawked at me like I was being rude.

"I mean, I didn't see any other cars on the road," I added with a lighter lift in my voice.

"Oh, I came in from the other side." He pointed back beyond the far buildings. "From the agricultural fields. It's where they grew all their own food. You know, for the asylum. It housed over two thousand patients at its height. Major overcrowding."

I could tell he was overloaded with details about the place and wanting to share them. It was clear he'd been studying it for some time. But I couldn't shake my distress from the vision of the dead woman, and I needed to get away from him so I could talk to Kaitlin.

"Well, nice to meet you," I said. "I think we'll just walk around and explore a bit."

He shifted his weight to the other foot. "All right. You'll see the women's wards along the right side of the grounds." He pointed to a row of buildings along the road. "The Excited Ward, the Convulsing Ward, the Untidy Ward, and the Quiet Ward. The men's wards are along the other side, identical." He pointed his arm in the other direction. "The infirmary is the one down there with the raised roof. They believed the sicknesses would rise and leave the building through the vaulted ceiling."

My eyes widened with interest. He did know a lot about the place.

He continued, "And the high-security ward, Ward B, is at the back with the fencing around it. That was where the most dangerous and volatile patients were sent." He paused. "The first floor was triage. The second floor was suicide watch."

"Wow. Quite a history to this place," Braden said, studying each building as if they would start telling their own stories at any moment.

Hooking onto Kaitlin's elbow, I started walking. "Okay, we'll be sure to have a look. Thanks." And trying not to appear too rude, I continued moving away from the group with Kaitlin in hopes the guys would follow.

Braden's face showed surprise that I didn't want to hear more from this man. Nick had stopped listening halfway through, which was typical of his attention span. Braden reached forward, then shook the guy's hand.

"Thanks. I'm Braden," he said.

"I'm Tom Johnson," the man replied, gripping Braden's hand. "I actually used to work here, some twenty years ago, when the last of the men's wards were still open. Let me know if you have any questions. I'll be here for a little while more." He passed a business card to him.

"Thanks, man. And these are my...." Braden stopped, realizing we'd already stepped away. He shrugged and then hurried to catch up to us.

Squeezing my eyes shut, I shook my head. Maybe my mind had been playing tricks on me. Maybe it was my head injury. I turned to Kaitlin, examining her ashen face.

"You saw it, too?" I whispered.

She pressed her lips together as if refusing to speak.

"Kaitlin. Did you see her?" I repeated.

She nodded once.

I covered my mouth with a shaky hand as she confirmed the vision I'd seen of the woman hanging from the tree.

"Shit." I dropped her elbow from mine, then stepped away from her. "What the fuck *was* that?"

Kaitlin blinked as if trying to wash away what she had seen. "Let's go," she said. "I want to go home."

"Maybe it was just our minds playing tricks on us," I said. "I mean, that guy, Tom...he was in the background walking toward us when we saw her. Maybe it was a strange trick of the light coming through the branches, mixed with the movement of him approaching."

It was possible. It was one potential explanation. And it was certainly more rational than our initial interpretation.

"Do you think so?" Kaitlin asked.

I shot a look back toward the tree to see if it could be a real possibility. Maybe the light was still hitting it in a way that would illuminate Tom again.

But my attention jumped to a new situation that raised my flight response again.

Tom was gone.

∼

I frantically searched in every direction to find where Tom might have gone. He'd just disappeared.

"Where'd he go?" I blurted, searching the entire area.

Braden turned, scanning the location we'd just walked away from.

"He must be behind one of the buildings or something." He looked back at me. "Did he freak you out?"

"No, I just…" I hesitated, searching for my words so I wouldn't sound crazy. "I just looked back and poof, he was gone."

"He's just a history nerd," Nick interjected. "We could take him, no problem." He jabbed at Braden's arm.

I glanced at the tree and all around it. He'd stepped out of sight so quickly, but Braden was right. He was probably just behind a building or something.

"Let's check out the high-security ward," Nick said. "I want to see where they put the psychos. I bet it's haunted."

Braden turned to me to see if I wanted to go.

"I don't know," I said. "I think Kaitlin's ready to get out of here."

"*Noo*. We have to check it out," Nick whined.

"Dude," Braden said with a firm tone. "The girls are hurt. Just because you can't see it doesn't mean their injuries don't exist."

Nick kicked at the dirt, put his hands in his pockets. "Fine. But I'm coming back here," he added. "I want to break into one of these buildings and see what's inside."

Braden glanced back to where Tom had been. "Yeah, maybe when that guy's gone. He probably wouldn't appreciate us violating his asylum."

I had to admit, breaking into one of the buildings had crossed my mind as well. Numerous times since we'd entered the grounds. And I knew it was more than a whim. It was a necessity. A new obsession. I had to see inside one. Or all of them.

"Do you think it would be possible?" I asked. "You know…to break into one?"

Braden's eyes widened. "Seriously? You'd want to?"

"Yeah." I nodded. "Definitely."

I raised an eyebrow at Kaitlin. "How about you?"

She lifted her drooped head, catching my eye. Fear radiated from her pupils, causing my heart rate to increase double-time. But then she nodded and said, "Yeah. I need to."

"What do you mean 'you need to'?" Nick asked with a cynical tone.

"I mean, I'm curious," Kaitlin clarified. "I can't leave without seeing inside one."

"I thought you wanted to get out of here, like, now," I said.

She shot her eyes all around us to be sure we were alone. "I've got a little bit left in me. Let's just poke around a tiny bit more."

I chewed my bottom lip and thought of wandering through the grounds more. Maybe we would find a weak spot in one of the boards or a door with a padlock that might not be fully secured. Anything was possible in such a big place.

We walked along the road that trailed in front of the women's wards. Each red-brick building held a unique shape, but they displayed similar architectural style. One had pointed gables and small windows, while another was squarer and more ivy-covered.

We passed in front of the one with the slate-tiled gables, and my body stiffened. My arms dragged with a weight that felt like sandbags hanging from my wrists. I slowed my pace, then stopped directly in front of the building and stared at it.

The weight continued to pull on my arms as a strange feeling of intense sadness moved through me. The sadness filled my neck, making it impossible to swallow or speak. Pushing my mouth open, I forced out the only sound I could conjure.

"*Ackk.*" The ache in my broken voice frightened me.

"Grace," Braden called. "What is it?" He launched to my side and shook my shoulder.

The power in his grip jolted the feeling of immense sadness out of me, and I took a deep gasp of air. Turning to Kaitlin, I froze in terror as I took her in.

She stood with her shoulders dropped low, as if pulled down by a great weight, and she gazed at the front door of the gabled building in terror. Her mouth propped open as if trying to speak but there were no words, only a familiar spine-tingling sound I couldn't unhear.

Misery in her voice grated out of her. "*Ackk.*"

CHAPTER 5

There was something odd about the building. An uncomfortable, excited energy that unnerved me. Something sinister.
And it had its hooks in Kaitlin, too.
I grabbed onto her arm, then yanked her away from the gabled ward. She shook her head as she stumbled along with me.
"I feel like I'm trapped in a bad dream," she said. "What is this place? It's like it's haunted or something."
"I know. I feel it, too," I agreed. "It's like the souls here are still in torment or something. The unsettled energy is crazy."
Braden stepped closer. "You guys are kinda freakin' me out. Are you connecting with paranormal vibes or something? Do we need to bring the ghost-hunters in?"
I ran my fingers through my hair, attempting to look as normal as possible in such an abnormal situation. Braden was noticing our odd behavior, and his confused reaction was my gauge. If he thought we were acting weird, then we were. Maybe my head injury was worse than I'd realized. Particularly if I couldn't hide its symptoms from my friends.
"Don't worry, Braden," I said in a lighter tone. "We're just having fun. We love this freaky stuff. You know that."

Kaitlin frowned, and I shot a glare at her to get her to play along with my farce. She caught my signal, then nodded in understanding. I nearly rolled my eyes at her lag time for not keeping up with my thought process, wondering if her concussion was to blame.

Although, I still couldn't understand why my own injury felt so... good. I'd never felt smarter or clearer in all my life. Like a new doorway had been opened. One that invited me into its secret realm.

As we walked a few paces away from the gabled ward, a strange high-pitched sound turned all of our heads toward the middle of the grounds. We stared at a long, one-story building with the loading dock that ran across the front of it. Then the sound faded.

"What the hell was that?" Nick stopped in his tracks.

We shifted and changed our direction, as if by instinct, and walked toward the plain building. My eyes narrowed as I studied its features, devoid of architectural beauty, possibly built after the original brick buildings, and wondered what it could be.

"Let's check it out," Braden said as he picked up his pace.

We crossed the green and passed a row of mature black maples. The thick trunks and sturdy branches hinted at their proud status as original occupants to the institution—their stories held tight within the rings of their dense wood.

I kept my eyes set forward for fear of seeing another image of a person hanging from the regal boughs. It was a gruesome sight I hoped to never see again.

We approached the long building, moving toward the cement stairs that led up to the platform of the loading dock. Like a porch, it ran along the entire front of the building. Braden hopped up the steps. In two strides, he was on the deck. He edged along the platform, surveying the main entrance, which was tightly padlocked.

My eyes shot to the side of the building in response to a rattling sound—metal banging on metal with a clanging vibration.

"What the hell?" I gasped.

Braden hopped down from the front of the dock, and the four of us snuck around to the side of the building, following the strange sound. As we rounded the corner, our feet sank in a thin layer of black

THE SHUTTERED WARD

mud that covered the pavement. In a gradual downward slope of the asphalt, the mud thickened at the bottom and oozed up the sides of our shoes.

"Try to walk around it," I said. "It only gets deeper over here." I pointed toward the edge of the building and then I fell silent.

At the bottom edge of the building, the foundation was exposed. Crumbling cracked concrete led to a metal grate—a vent of some sort. A large piece of plywood leaned against the vent in a makeshift attempt at holding it in place. The screws of the metal grate had come loose from their concrete housing, and the iron frame rattled whenever the plywood caught the slightest breeze.

The vent was expansive. Big enough even for Braden to pass through.

I crouched, peering into the darkness behind the grate. It led to a crawl space below the building. Maybe there was access to the inside from under there. My skin prickled with excitement.

"Should we try to squeeze in?" I pulled on the edge of the metal screen.

"Shit," Nick complained. "We'll get dirty." He looked at us to see if we were seriously considering going into the rotting crawl space. "These are my good shoes." He glanced at the bright white of his new Vans.

"Dude, it's worth it," Braden said. "It's just asking for us to go in." He pulled the plywood away from the opening.

Yanking along the edges of the metal covering, I found the bottom corner to be the weakest. I was able to pull it away from the edge of the building just far enough for someone to squeeze in.

With a grin, I said, "Who's first?"

∽

Everyone regarded me like I was insane.

"Fine," I said. "I'll go first." I waved for Braden to step closer to hold the metal covering for me. "Keep it pulled open. And Nick, shine your flashlight in there. I need to see what I'm heading into."

Nick pulled his phone from his pocket. "It's gonna drain my battery."

"Just do it," I said as I bent for a better look in.

Kaitlin squeezed up behind me. "What if we get caught?"

I shot a glance toward the green, searching for any sign of Tom, then pushed through the opening. My shirt snagged on the jagged edge of the metal caging, tearing slightly, and the knees of my jeans grew wet from the damp flooring. I crawled in farther. "Come on. Kaitlin. You next."

She bounced in place, contemplating the derelict building. "But there's a sign over there. It says hazardous."

"We'll be careful," I called. "Come on. It's creepy in here alone." I twisted to see behind me, half-expecting a rabid raccoon to hiss at me or a decomposing corpse to grab me.

The crawl space went under only a small portion of the building. A few oversized cylinders were piled in the corner.

"Shine your light over there." I pointed for Nick. The beam sent a dull glow toward the packaging materials, and I saw black stenciled lettering on the brown cylinders that read '**Blackwood State Hospital**'. Burlap bags lay all around them, shredded, probably by rats. I grimaced at the thought of stumbling onto a rat's nest. I'd rather bump into a decaying zombie.

"I'm coming in next," Braden called.

Kaitlin continued to fidget at the grate, while Nick aimed his flashlight at us.

I crawled farther in to make room for him, then scooched closer to the pile of cylinder containers. A shiny tin hatch was positioned directly above the pile, and I turned to Braden with wide eyes.

"There's a door," I whispered. "Like a laundry shoot."

Braden struggled within the small space, cursing as he awkwardly dragged himself closer.

"Where?" He glanced up from his efforts for a quick look.

I pulled myself over the cardboard barrels, then pressed on the tin hatch. It rattled loosely on its hinges. "Here!"

Braden examined the potential access point before whispering for

Kaitlin and Nick to follow. I squatted under the metal cover, then pushed up on it fully. It was light, and it bowed and banged from my efforts. With little resistance, it opened up into the floor above.

I stared back at Braden with my mouth open.

"Can you see in?" he asked as he crawled closer.

I stood taller so I could lift my eyes just above the opening to see where it might lead. The fear of vermin jumping at my face was my primary concern, then maybe decapitation from a random ax-wielder just waiting for a stupid person to poke their head up into their lair.

In absolute silence, I scanned the area above the hatch and saw more barrels stacked around the opening, set on loose linoleum-tiled flooring. Glass-block windows flooded the area with light, and enormous stainless-steel appliances lined the walls. A waft of stale, moldy air hit me, causing my nose to itch.

"It's like an old kitchen," I whispered to Braden. "Help me up."

"Come on, guys," he called to the others. "We're going in."

"What the fuck?" Nick grumbled. "This is disgusting." He glanced around the dirty crawlspace with a grimace.

"Don't be a pussy," Braden shot back. "Just get in here."

Kaitlin sent a worried glance my way. She wasn't the most athletic or agile, and it was clear this part of the mission was not her favorite.

"It's fine, Kaitlin," I reassured her. "Just climb on one of those barrels and hoist yourself up."

"I'll help you," Braden added.

With a nod, she crept farther into the crawlspace.

In no time, the four of us pushed our way through the grain shoot and into the kitchen. Braden was the last to pull himself up, being the tallest. And, okay, the most muscular.

The sour smell of mildew thickened the air, and I wished we had bandanas to wrap around our faces. But I was quickly distracted by the abrupt throwback to an earlier time period. The interior decor was like a show from the sixties, or earlier. The space was mostly empty, but the remains of high-volume food production were all around—huge silver appliances and sinks along the back, a conveyor for sliding trays along, and thick white doors with rounded edges and silver handles for walk-in refrigeration.

We moved around the industrial facility as our movement and voices echoed through the building. I peered into a doorway that opened into a huge space, like a cafeteria, with brown-tiled flooring, peeling white walls, and a crumbling ceiling. Beyond the wide space were several dark halls shooting off the back.

I glanced at Braden. He lifted his eyebrows, gesturing at the dark corridors. But in that same moment, a strange sound traveled out from the darkness, causing prickles to lift on the nape of my neck. It was a high-pitched screeching sound that rose and fell, then faded away.

I turned to Kaitlin. Her eyes wide as saucers, and she shook her head in micro-shakes in a terrified posture of refusal.

"It's okay, Kaitlin," I said. "It's just an old building, like a dining hall. At least it's not where they did the lobotomies and shit." I huffed, trying to lighten her mood. But honestly, this place creeped me out, too. It didn't matter it was the food service building. It still held its own morbid secrets and haunting mysteries.

"I don't like it in here," she said. "And that sound. What the hell is that?" She stared into the darkness of the corridors. "It's like someone's trapped. Tortured. Just wailing."

Her words sent chills along my skin, and I listened for it again. The silence calmed me. But then, the eerie sound returned, and my flight response tensed my muscles.

But something else was stronger. The urge to explore. To find whatever it was that drew us here. My mind flashed with images of the dark corridors and what they might hold—more dining rooms, storages, unknown alcoves. Ghosts, even.

Before I realized it, I was across the dining hall, standing at the passageways to the back halls, waving for the other to join me.

∼

I reached through Kaitlin's elbow as we entered the darkness of the middle corridor. Our footsteps echoed through the deep hall as we crunched across fallen plaster and bits of debris. The light from the glass-block windows faded behind us. Now the only illumination that entered the space was from the edges of the boarded-up windows. I searched for weakness or gaps of light, keeping alert to any possible escape routes.

We moved through the dark hallway, glancing into side rooms, half expecting a ghoul to jump out at any moment. Some rooms had metal tables or sinks, and others held old boxes. The corridor snaked and turned deeper into the building, leading us to random open spaces.

"Check this out," Nick said.

We gathered at the opening to a side room where he stood and poked in. Everything in the space was shiny tin—a table in the center and counters along the sides, a runner along the ceiling with huge sharp hooks, and a tall spike at the side of the room pointing directly up from the floor.

My heart dropped as I stared at the horrible devices of torture. "What the hell is this?" My voice trembled as I cowered at the doorway.

Nick shined his light around the space, illuminating the shiny metal surfaces, and stepped into the room.

"Don't go in there," I blurted. "It looks dangerous." My voice shook.

"It looks like a butcher's workroom," Braden said.

I exhaled for miles. He was right. I'd allowed my imagination to run away with me, losing sight of the obvious. But still, I inched back away from the view of the sharp metal objects, which were likely used to rip carcasses apart.

Leaning back, I gazed down toward a larger space that opened up at the end of the hall. Light glowed in the area, welcoming me closer to it. I pulled on Kaitlin to follow me, and she peered toward the space with a skeptical glare.

We stepped toward the room, drawn by the light, and I turned to the guys. "Come this way, there's…" But my voice stuck in my neck.

They were gone. Vanished.

"Braden?" I whispered. "Nick?" I clamped onto Kaitlin's arm. "It's not funny, you guys. Cut the shit."

We stood like statues in silence, straining to hear any clue of which direction they'd gone.

"You guys are assholes," Kaitlin whimpered.

My heart pounded in my ears as I scanned the corridor we'd just come through. We'd taken so many turns, I wasn't sure I could find our way back. I checked my phone, and it was at seventeen percent. My flashlight was draining it fast.

"What's your charge?" I asked Kaitlin.

She glanced at her phone. "Three percent."

"Shit!" I turned my light off. "Let's use yours until it runs out. Then we'll switch to mine."

"Grace...?" Kaitlin's voice squeaked out of her.

Her lost tone proved she didn't know what to do next.

"Just stay close to me," I said. Then I made myself call out, "You guys. Cut the crap. Get back here!" My voice echoed throughout the empty spaces, then bounced back to me with no evidence of where they might have gone. "They're just screwing with us," I said. "Come on. Two can play that game."

I pulled Kaitlin toward the glowing light of the large room. We entered the stagnant space, and Kaitlin turned her flashlight off. There was enough light to see the shadows of items around the room. Broken chairs, overturned trash cans, and parts of a table. In the center of the room was a massive pile of dirty, soggy chunks of plaster and insulation. I stepped closer to it, then looked up. A gaping hole in the ceiling spilled its guts all over the floor, reminding me of the infirm condition of the condemned building.

My eyes followed the strongest beams of light, landing on the boarded-up windows at the rear of the room. As I glanced around to find the brightest glow, my hair stood on end as the familiar screeching sound pierced through my soul.

Kaitlin jumped like a frightened cat. "Jesus," she screamed.

The sound hit a rapid high pitch that then turned into a slower drone of pain and misery. Like someone being tortured.

My eyes filled with tears of sorrow as a heavy weight pushed down on me—the weight of intense, deep sadness. It filled my throat, making it difficult to speak or even breathe.

Frozen in place, I moved my eyes to the side to see Kaitlin. Tears fell from her open eyes, and she trembled all over.

"I'm trapped," she murmured.

"What?"

"I can't move," she said.

I forced my eyes toward the light from the boarded window, then back to Kaitlin. The heavy weight pulled at my hands, dragging my shoulders down. I fought it, but it was so hard.

"I feel it, too," I whispered. "Fight it, Kaitlin."

"But I'm tired," she said as she slowly dropped to her knees.

"No," I shouted. "Stay up!" Fighting against the weight of heavy sadness, I grabbed Kaitlin by the shoulders. "Up! Come on. We're breaking out of here!"

~

I dragged Kaitlin past the wet mash that had fallen out of the broken ceiling, but the screeching all around us grew louder.

"Grab that trash can." I pushed Kaitlin toward a pile of debris near the boarded windows.

I rummaged through the broken furniture, then pulled a wooden chair leg out of the hoard. Kaitlin dragged a metal can over, scraping and banging enough to rattle my bones.

"Shh. Don't give away our location." I hushed her with my hands, then took the handle of the metal can. I spun it to find the least dented side, imagining curious trash collection guys smashing it repeatedly against a garbage truck to empty its contents, while vying for a glimpse of the lunatics. Then I flipped it over and pushed the strongest side under the window.

I slid a wooden box up to the base of the can, then stepped on it. With the broken chair leg in hand, I hoisted myself onto the top of the trash can.

"Hold me steady," I said to Kaitlin. "Grab my legs."

When I stood on the can, it wobbled under my weight. Steadying myself, I felt along the bottom of the plywood board that covered the window. Its screws had come loose from the concrete window jambs, and the entire board flapped outward.

"Shit. We can get out this way," I whispered. "You first, Missy!"

Kaitlin scrambled onto the box, then awkwardly pulled her knees up to the top of the can. She struggled to balance, so I reached for her hand and pulled her up to standing.

"I hate when you call me that," she said as she held the window frame to steady herself.

"No you don't," I said. "You love it."

She rolled her eyes, and I chuckled. Her mother called her 'Missy' once, and she'd gone crazy. I couldn't help but keep it going. Especially at a time like this.

"How am I going to fit through that?" When she pressed the board outward, it opened a few inches.

I took the wooden chair leg, using it to prop the opening. Like a crowbar, I pushed down and watched it wedge the board open, loosening screws halfway up the height of the window. I pulled the chair leg out, then propped the board open with it.

"Just slide through now," I said. "Then hang from your hands as low as possible…and drop."

She hopped up to the ledge to peer out. "It's just grass. That's good."

"You got this." I wove my fingers together, telling her to put her foot in my hands. "I'll give you a boost."

Once her foot was cradled in my hands, I hoisted her up farther. She wiggled, her butt swaying from side to side like a stuck animal, and I burst out laughing. My legs crossed to keep from peeing myself, and I worried I'd fall from the can.

"Bitch," Kaitlin shouted, wriggling non-stop.

I cracked up more as I pushed her out the window. In a slow-motion fall, her weight carried her out the opening and she fell down the side of the building as she clung on to the window ledge.

"Now drop," I coached her.

Her fingers released. With a thud, she landed below.

"Come on," she squealed. "Hurry."

I looked behind me, sure an entity would be hovering, waiting to grab me and pull me into the abyss of insanity. Panic filled my every muscle. The sound of the screeching shot terror through me, and I jumped at the window. I shimmied until I hung at my waist, halfway in, halfway out.

Kaitlin reached for me from below. "Come on!"

Gripping the sill, I pulled my legs up. Something was going to grab my ankle and yank me back in. I was sure of it. And I struggled to get my body out of there. Before I could get a grip, my legs followed me out the window and their weight pulled me off the ledge. I fell with a thud. Right on top of Kaitlin.

She squirmed beneath me, then pushed me off. We searched each other for signs of injury. At the same moment, we burst out laughing. It was a release of terror. And of immense sadness. And tears poured from our eyes from the depth of the laughter and the relief.

"Oh my God," I babbled. "I can't believe we…"

My words were cut off from the echoing call of our names from within the building.

"Grace!"

"Kaitlin!"

CHAPTER 6

Braden and Nick's panicked voices boomed through the interior of the dining hall. They'd clearly expected to find us cowering in a corner, whimpering for their rescue.

But hell no.

We'd got our asses out of there, and it was their turn to be pranked.

"Let's go." I jumped up, grabbing for Kaitlin's hand. "Let's get to the green and hide behind a tree. They'll freak when they can't find us."

"I feel bad," Kaitlin whined.

"They ditched us first, Kaitlin," I barked. "They deserve a little payback."

She nodded and allowed me to pull her up, assisting me as little as possible.

We ran around the side of the dining facility and out to the open lawn area. I glanced at the tree that spooked us earlier, deciding to go in the opposite direction. I stopped at the base of a tree that's branches all pointed upward, leaving no possibility of having ever been used for a hanging.

I pulled Kaitlin behind me. We hovered behind the thick trunk, peeking out for any sign of the boys exiting the building.

"Any second now," I whispered, staring at the side where we had originally crept in.

Then, as if a bomb detonated in my brain, the sound of a man's voice spun me around with a shock that loosened my bones.

"Hide and seek?" His voice bounced around in my shattered skull.

"Jesus!" I huffed. "You scared the shit out of me."

I struggled to regain my composure. He pushed his glasses up the bridge of his nose. "Sorry. I didn't mean to startle you."

I pulled in a full breath to try to see straight again. "No, sorry. I didn't mean to swear," I apologized. He seemed too proper to be sworn at, and I felt guilty. "You just took us by surprise."

"Yeah, this place can do that to a person," he said. "You know, make you jumpy."

"I guess." I swiveled toward Kaitlin only to find she hadn't recovered from the fright yet. Her face was sheet white, and she panted while holding her hand at her heart. I nearly burst out laughing again for lack of any other appropriate response.

"Where are your friends?" he asked, looking in the direction of the dining hall.

"Oh, they're right over there. Exploring," I answered, making it seem like they'd be rejoining us any second.

"Well, they won't find much there," he said. "Most of the activity happens here, behind you." He pointed to the row of wards at our backs.

"Activity?" I repeated.

"Yeah. Like paranormal stuff," he said. "You know, hauntings. Is that not what you guys are looking for?"

My eyes widened with intrigue. "Well, not exactly. We didn't even know this place existed until today."

"Really?" He studied my face to be sure I wasn't messing with him. "Could have fooled me."

"Hmm?" My head tipped.

What the hell was he talking about? First, he was some scholarly, historical dude. Now he was an investigator questioning our purpose for being there.

"I don't know," he added. "Just seems like you might have other intentions." He shrugged.

Maybe he thought we were there to vandalize the place. Or to break in. He wasn't far off then. I guessed if he were the groundskeeper, then it made sense he'd be protective of it.

I glanced back for any sign of the guys. Tom seemed nice, but he still was a stranger and creeped me out.

"The wards are worth having a look at. That's the Excited Ward over there." He pointed to the building we'd stopped in front of earlier. The one Kaitlin and I'd frozen at.

"Why is it called the Excited Ward?" I asked, gazing at its deteriorating steps and decrepit front entry.

"It's where the unstable women were sent. And the violent, unruly ones. The ones who had to be strapped to the beds with restraints."

"That's messed up," Kaitlin mumbled.

Tom pointed to the building next to it. "That's the Convulsing Ward. The epileptics and women with seizures were housed there. They were thought to be possessed at the time, probably." He turned to the building on the other side of the Excited Ward. "And that's the Untidy Ward. For women who needed help with...personal hygiene."

"What?" Kaitlin asked with the corner of her lip raised.

He hesitated. "Women who soiled themselves or made a mess of it. That sort of thing," he muttered, turning away from our gazes. I was sure he blushed.

"That's nuts," I said, staring at each building, imagining the women who would be assigned to each one. "Who made the decisions on where each prisoner would be locked up?"

"Patients," Tom said.

"What?" I shook my head.

"Patients. Not prisoners."

"Oh, right. That's what I meant," I clarified apologetically. I was a little surprised by his sensitive reaction to the word *prisoner*, even among the condemned buildings of an old insane asylum.

"The patients would be evaluated by the superintendent at the administration building over there." Tom pointed toward where we first entered the grounds. "Depending on their level of violence."

"Violence?" I repeated.

"Many of the patients were criminally insane—sent here for murdering their own parents or killing their children. But most were just misdiagnosed and given prescriptions for the most advanced medical practices of the time. You know, shock therapy and lobotomies."

"That's actually terrifying," I interjected. "I can't even imagine it."

"Well, you don't have to. You…" His voice trailed off as shouting came from the other direction.

Braden and Nick came barreling toward us, yelling our names.

"What the fuck?" Nick shouted. "How the hell did you get out here?"

They hurried over to us, panting with frantic expressions strewn across their faces.

"You scared the shit out of us," Braden said. "Grace," he panted. "I didn't know what happened to you."

As I stared into his wild eyes, guilt washed over me. "What? You guys abandoned *us*. What did you expect?"

He reached out to touch my hair, but he stopped himself. Again, he reached for my arm, but stopped. "You scared the shit out of me."

"Yeah, you said that already," I teased. "But you tried to scare the shit out of us first. On purpose!" I stared at him with accusing eyes.

"It was just a joke," he said. "We hid in one of the refrigerators, then waited for you guys to turn back and search for us."

"We were gonna jump out and watch you scream your heads off," Nick added.

"Well, you should know us better than that," I said. "We're more resourceful than you think. If you're looking for damsels in distress, you should hang out with Cammie and Lauren."

Kaitlin chuckled. We hated Cammie and Lauren. They got all the guys because they faked being dumb and giggled at every word the boys said. It was infuriating. But they were also known for handing out free blow jobs, so that gave us a little vindication anyway.

Braden rolled his eyes, then scanned the dirt on my shirt and the fresh rip in the knee of my jeans. "Sorry. I didn't mean for it to go like that." He glared at Nick, clearly feeling bad for following along with his trick.

"It's okay," I said. "Whatever."

"Did you guys hear the crazy screaming in there?" Kaitlin leaned in, nearly falling forward.

"What the fuck? Yes," Nick shouted. "That scared the shit out of me. I thought someone was being killed. By slow torture."

Tom stepped closer, reminding us he was even there. "That's the weather vane at the top of the bakery. The orderlies used to call it the 'Mascot of the Laughing Academy'." He pointed to the peak of the historic brick building attached to the side of the dining facility. "It spins with the gusts. The stronger the wind, the faster it moves. Hasn't been oiled in decades, so yeah, it squeaks and well, screams, you could say."

I stared at the rusted weather vane that leaned, crooked, off the highest gable of the building. I hated it. It had scarred my soul with a profound fear that settled permanently deep in my bones. I'd never felt such terror, and I would never forget it.

"What does that mean? Laughing Academy?" I asked Tom.

"You know, it was insulting slang, like 'loony bin' or 'funny farm'. Ignorance, really." He shrugged.

A gentle breeze rustled the leaves in the tree above us. It picked up in strength, and I watched the branches sway. Moving my gaze back to the weather vane, I waited.

The wind blew harder.

The weather vane remained silent.

I shot a perplexed gaze back at Tom.

But he was gone again.

～

I searched in every direction, frantic to find where Tom had gone and

THE SHUTTERED WARD

exhaled in relief as I saw him strolling down the road toward a different building. **Ward B**, its fading sign said.

My natural instinct was to follow him. I took a few steps in his direction, but Kaitlin grabbed on to me.

"Stop," she begged. "I can't. I need to get home now."

I kept my eyes fixed on Tom.

"Please, Grace." She tugged on my arm.

Braden stepped up next to me. "I think she's right," he said. "You guys need to rest. It's been a lot."

"Pretty cool, though," Nick added. "You have to admit."

Kaitlin and Braden *were* right. It was time to go. Too much had happened. Too many complex ideas were blasting through my mind. I couldn't organize all the racing thoughts and flashing images that spiraled in my head. I just needed to rest. To settle everything around me so I could focus on the immense concepts bouncing around in my skull.

"Yeah, okay," I agreed. Swiveling toward Tom, I yelled, "Bye, Tom! Thank you." And I waved. But he didn't flinch or turn around to us. He just kept walking toward Ward B. I shrugged. "Let's go."

We walked along the cracked, crumbling road back toward the drive we entered from. I stared at the administration building near the entryway, and chills ran through me as I imagined what it would be like to be evaluated in there. The struggles of adolescence alone were enough to get someone sectioned back then.

Crying for no understood reason, explosive emotions, defiance to social expectations, sexual curiosity—they were all acceptable reasons back then, to get a girl sent away against her will. I actually felt bad for any of the girls who were sent to the asylum. Clearly, their parents hadn't understood what they were going through. Possession, witchcraft, or insanity were the easiest explanations for teen angst in the early 1900s.

I studied the front door to the admin building. Its crumbling concrete steps barely held their form. The wooden architectural decor fell away from the moldings, but they were still held strong by solid white pillars. Then my attention snapped to a featureless building next to it. Set near the chapel. Devoid of any architectural detail, it emanated anguish and suffering.

My head tipped for a better look, but then a piercing pain shot through my skull. I squinted my eyes, pressing my fingers on them to stop the deep ache behind them. It felt as if the nerves behind my eyes were on fire. 'Ocular headaches' my doctor called them—to be expected from recovering head trauma.

I scurried to catch up to the others, but I couldn't help myself from gazing back at the ominous building. It scared me. Like it knew I had discovered its presence, but it wanted to remain unseen. A sinister feeling moved through my body, and I feared for any girl who ever had to enter it. Her terror must have been unreal.

"We need to come back here again," Braden said. "This place is cool."

"I'll bring my dab pen," Nick added. "Imagine this place high."

Jesus. That was the last thing I'd ever do here. It blew my mind enough sober. I'd lose my sanity if I ever came here high.

I glanced at Kaitlin, and she shook her head at me as if saying, "Hell no."

I nodded in agreement, ready to leave all of this far behind us. I was officially exhausted and shaken to the core. Something had rattled me. Deeply. And I was left with a sense of disturbance that unsettled my soul.

It was as if there was a presence here. An entity that wanted to make itself known. It pulled at me, drawing my attention to doorways of specific buildings.

I needed to come back to understand it better, but I squeezed my eyes shut in resistance. But it was too late. My mind was already made up.

I was coming back here again with Kaitlin. Only Kaitlin.

∽

The guys rambled nonstop on the drive home, recapping every detail of the visit to the asylum, while Kaitlin and I sat silently in the back-

THE SHUTTERED WARD

seat. We stared ahead with blank expressions like we were traumatized. We'd pushed ourselves too far. We needed rest or we'd regress in our recoveries, or so we were told. But rest was the last thing I wanted to do.

Braden pulled up to my house, and Kaitlin and I climbed out.

"Thanks, guys," I said with the last bit of energy I could muster. "That was…" I searched for the right word. "Unexpected."

"See ya later," Braden called before driving off.

Kaitlin and I dragged ourselves up the front walk toward my door, then I noticed my mother's car in the driveway.

"Shit! My mother's home," I grumbled.

Before we even set foot on the porch, the door flew open.

"Where the hell have you been?" she blasted. "Why haven't you responded to my texts?"

When I pulled my phone out of my pocket, I realized it was dead.

"Sorry, Mom," I said. "My phone died, I guess."

"And you turned your tracking off?" She glared.

"Oh, I forgot about that." I shook my head in confusion. She was throwing too much energy at me, and I was beyond spent. "I'll turn it back on."

I preferred to keep my tracking off. She was the only one who truly stalked me. And today, I hadn't even wanted her to know I'd left the house. Let alone embarked on a full-blown haunted adventure.

"You're supposed to be resting," she stated. "Kaitlin, I'm sorry, but you'll have to go home now. You should be in bed, too, you know."

Kaitlin dropped her eyes to the ground. My mother intimidated her, and she could hardly look her in the eye. Ever.

Before long, Kaitlin's mom arrived and took her home. But not before we'd agreed to Facetime later. We had a ridiculous amount to talk about, but not with our mothers anywhere nearby.

I made a move to go hide in my room, but Mom stopped me.

"Look at me," she said.

I lifted my reluctant gaze to hers as if being inspected by a warden.

"Your eyes are bloodshot," she said. "Have you been smoking that funny stuff again? It's of the devils, you know. Meant to distract you and create deviance."

"No, Mom." I couldn't keep the annoyance out of my voice. "I'm not high. I don't smoke weed. I've told you that."

"Then why are your eyes so red?" She leaned in for a better look.

"I'm tired. I'm concussed. I have a headache the size of Jupiter," I said with as much snark as possible.

"Well, I told you that you should be resting," she shot back.

Her shrill voice cut into my brain, toppling me over the edge. Bending, I smacked my hands over my eyes to stop the blinding light from entering them. It was like two red hot pokers were driving through my eyeballs into my brain. I screamed out in mind-numbing pain.

"Grace…" my mother called from what seemed like a million miles away. "What is it?" she cried out.

I writhed on the floor, pressing my hands against my eyes. For a moment, I swiped my hands away and tried to blink through the pain. In a blast of pure terror, I saw only darkness.

"Mom! I can't see," I screamed.

"Holy Jesus, I'm calling 911!" And her voice faded in and out as I begged for someone to help me.

CHAPTER 7

My eyelids flickered from the bright light that taunted them. The pain behind my eyes was gone, and my jaw had unclenched from its vice grip. I prayed I would never feel that level of pain again in my entire life. Then I remember the blindness and my eyes shot open.

Light poured into my pupils, and images of a hospital room filled my sight. Tears poured from the relief that overwhelmed me. I was okay. I was safe.

"Mom?" My voice squeaked out of me.

"Oh, thank Christ." Her voice came from the far corner of the room where she'd been resting in the vinyl armchair. She barreled over to me, staring deeply into my eyes. "Thank Jesus and the grace of God."

"I'm okay," I mumbled, already annoyed by her holy-roller comments. "How long have I been here?"

"Overnight," she said. "It's lunchtime now. They gave you a sedative, and you slept. They took an MRI, but the results were normal." She paused. "They say your head injury caused the temporary blindness. Like an intense migraine."

"Could it happen again?" I reached for my head and rubbed it.

"They say you need to rest," she said. "You overexerted yourself and brought it on."

I was sure she'd just been dying to say that last part. Like it was my own fault. She loved being right and having the last word. I was too tired to argue so I let her have that one. I was only glad it was over. Temporary blindness was terrifying, and I never, ever wanted to know that feeling again.

"When can I go home?" I asked.

"They want to keep you one more day for observation," she said. "Then, with God's help, you can go."

I dropped my head back on my pillow. An extra day of forced rest couldn't hurt, I supposed, but I'd definitely rather be in my own room.

"Does Kaitlin know?" I murmured.

"Yes. I called her mother," Mom said. "To be sure she kept a close eye on her. Wouldn't want the same thing happening to her, you know."

I knew she could see my exasperation splashed across my face. She always got too involved and loved making decisions for other people, giving direction at every turn.

I searched the side table for my phone.

"It's here." Mom dug in her purse, then pulled out a charger as well. "It probably needs to charge." She fumbled at the wall for a plug. "But the doctor says minimal screen time. So I'll keep it over…"

"No, Mom," I interrupted. "I'll keep it right here with me." I lightened my tone with my next breath. "But I'll be sure to only use it a little."

She hesitated about placing it within my reach but then gave in. "Fine. Keep the brightness on the lowest setting."

"Thanks, Mom." I knew she meant well, but she needed to take some time for self-examination, to see why so many people avoided her and well, just didn't want to be around her. Me included.

"I'll get the doctor." She stepped toward the half-open door. "She told me to alert someone when you woke."

The moment she was out the door, I powered up my phone. It took its time coming to life, but once it did, my notifications went

THE SHUTTERED WARD

crazy. A gazillion texts from Kaitlin as she begged me to reply. Then some from Braden checking in to see how I was. The last one from Kaitlin said, "Your mom called mine. I hope you're okay. I'll visit tomorrow."

My feet danced at the end of my bed. I'd love a visit from Kaitlin. We had so much to talk about still.

I texted her back. "Come now!"

The next hour was filled with me getting poked and checked by nurses and the doctor. Everyone seemed pleased with my stable condition to the point where Mom decided to go home for a while, after much encouragement from me. I told her I wanted to sleep for the rest of my time there.

Soon after everyone had found more interesting distractions, I sat in my bed, anxiously awaiting Kaitlin. And before long, my door creaked open and a balloon poked through first. Followed by an unexpected visitor.

Braden.

∼

Braden poked his head into my room, waiting for an invitation to come all the way in.

"Hi." I smiled, instinctively combing my hair with my fingers.

He stepped farther in, fumbling with the balloon as it blocked his way. "Hey." He swatted at the plump 'Get Well' balloon that was determined to come between us. "I wanted to check in on you," he said.

"Aww. That's sweet," I teased. "It's kind of dumb I'm here, though. I'm fine."

"Yeah, I know." He stood at the edge of my bed, fidgeting. "I just thought you could use some company." He looked everywhere but at me.

"I like the balloon." I smirked.

He followed the pink string in his hand, raising his head to see the floating greeting. "Okay. It's dumb. But I didn't want to walk in here empty-handed."

"No, really," I said. "I like it."

And I did. It was goofy and childish. But it was cute. And nice.

He hovered and shifted his weight from one foot to another.

"You can drag that chair over if you want." I pointed to a folding chair by the far wall.

"Oh, okay." When he went for the chair, the balloon got stuck on the edge of the open door. He pulled at it, and it tangled on the doorknob. "What the hell? This thing doesn't like me." He finally unraveled it and tied it to the end of my bed, stepping away as if it would try to get back to him.

He dragged the chair over, avoiding the hovering balloon, and sat by my bedside.

I glanced at his face as he kept his eyes on the balloon. He'd had a huge glow-up in the final year of high school, and I hadn't noticed until now. His handsome features were more mature and chiseled, and any signs of acne were long gone. My head tipped as I saw him in a new light.

Butterflies tickled at my stomach, and I quickly cleared my wandering thoughts. *What the hell?* It was Braden. I slapped myself back to reality.

"How did you even know I was here?" I asked.

He turned his attention from the balloon. "Kaitlin told me," he said. "She was a little freaked out, you could say."

"Figures." I tried to imagine what went down when my mother contacted hers. She probably panicked them about the blindness. "What'd she say?"

"I'm not sure," he said. "She was breathing hard into the phone, and she couldn't keep her thoughts straight. Like, she rambled the entire time."

"Typical Kaitlin," I added. "She gets a little hysterical sometimes."

"Yeah, that's a good way of putting it." He grinned, lifting his eyebrows.

He dropped his gaze and checked his phone. Then he scanned the room. There was something else on his mind, I was sure. He was always a bit nervous around me, but today was different. He was right on the edge, teetering.

"That was weird yesterday," I said.

He moved his gaze back to me and settled there. He pulled his chair a little closer. "Yeah. What the hell was that?"

"What do you mean? What part?" I asked.

"The part where you, you know…" He hesitated. "Left me."

"In the dining hall?" I asked. "That was for pure survival."

"No, that's not what I mean." He glanced out the window and then back at me. "The part where you were like, in a trance."

∽

My eyes widened as I considered how it must have looked to Braden when I had my strange visions at the asylum. My head had been playing tricks on me, causing me to stare at flashbacks that didn't exist, but to Braden, it probably appeared like I was possessed or something.

"That's embarrassing," I mumbled.

"What?" He sat up straighter. "No, it's not. It was just…weird."

"I think it's just my head. They said I'd need more time to rest," I tried to explain. "Like, I would have mini shutdowns, kind of."

I did my best to make sense of it, but I was just as confused as him. What I'd seen at the asylum haunted me. The vision of the girl hanging from the tree was scary, but the feelings that coursed through me were even worse. Feeling of deep sadness and despair. It had felt so real and strong. The feeling terrified me by its pure magnitude. It held the power to make someone not want to carry on. Escaping it was my primary focus.

He fixed on my eyes for a moment, causing me to feel self-conscious. What was he trying to see?

Just as I was about to pull my eyes away from his, the door swung open, blowing the balloon at us. Braden swatted at it as if it were attacking him, and I burst out laughing.

A nurse walked in, pushing a cart of medical equipment along with her. "Oh, I'm glad to see you're in good humor," she said. "Alert and laughing."

I smiled at her.

"You've made a good recovery, Grace," she added. "Your chart says you came in here in rough shape last night."

"Yeah, I don't remember much of it," I said.

"Just as well, I suppose." She took a pressure cuff off the cart, then clipped something to the end of my finger. After she wrapped the cuff around my arm, it began squeezing. "I just need to take your vitals. I'm sure it's all fine," she explained. "Open." She placed a thermometer in my mouth.

I rolled my eyes at Braden. He smirked and looked away.

"And is this your handsome boyfriend?" she asked, checking the reading from the thermometer.

My face blazed red hot. "No, he's a friend," I responded quickly.

"Mhmm," she mumbled as she pulled the cuff off my arm. "And how are you feeling now? Would you like the doctor to stop in?"

"I think I'm fine." I rubbed my head. "I don't know."

"Well, I'll be sure she checks in on you," she said. "She's a specialist for head injury and recovery, so you're in good hands." And then she left us.

I rubbed my head again as a pain behind my left eye throbbed. "Shit." I squeezed my eyes shut. "It better not be happening again. Turn the lights off," I said to Braden.

"What?" He stood up and hovered.

"The lights," I repeated. "They're probably too bright. Can you flick them off?"

He hopped to the switch at the door, then shut off the lights. The room remained bright with daylight, but at least the fluorescent glare was gone.

Then the pain hit harder, and I jolted. Gathering the sheets of my bed, I pulled them up around my face to block the glare. Darkness surrounded me, and I peeked one eye open. My vision filled in an instant with flashes of the asylum, only the buildings looked different. The windows weren't boarded up, and fresh white paint coated the moldings and pillars at the front stairs of the various wards. Squeezing my eyes shut to clear the images, I opened them again. Before I could stifle it, a small scream escaped my mouth as I came face to face with the hanging woman's purple grimace of strangulated death.

Braden jumped to my side, then grabbed hold of my arm. "Grace!"

I tried to respond to him, but I couldn't break out of the dream. My vision traveled down the broken paved road toward Ward B, stopping at the high-security fencing. I reached my fingers to the chain link, trying to weave them in to help me climb, but the links were too small. My fingers wouldn't fit in. Instead, I banged on the fencing, calling out, "Kaitlin! Where are you?"

My wailing voice filled my head and all the space around me. Over and over, I called for her, but no answer. The only sound that came to me was a man's deep, panicked voice.

"Nurse! Help," the voice boomed around me. "Come quickly! Grace needs help."

CHAPTER 8

This time, the pain behind my eyes remained. Like a stabbing that gouged into my brain, it pressed at the back of my eyeballs, aching. I didn't bother opening them. I knew where I was. The low beeping sound by the side of my bed, the glare of fluorescents above me, the smell of sterile alcohol wipes… I didn't need to see it all again.

I wondered how much time had passed, though, since Braden's visit and well, the visions. I shook my head in micro-beats, fighting off the humiliation. This walk of shame was worse than any morning after binge drinking at one of Nick's parties. But I didn't have alcohol to blame this time. It was all on me.

A long, loud exhale released from my lungs as I accepted my predicament. Braden thought I was nuts. Maybe I was. Kaitlin thought I was nuts. If so, then she was, too. Mom thought I was, well…deranged. What was new?

"Ah, you're waking up." A calming woman's voice filled the room. "I expected such. Your meds are wearing off. They offered you some relief, I hope?"

I flickered one eye open, surprised to see a casually dressed middle-aged woman who looked like she spent more time in the yoga studio than in a hospital. I nearly expected her to start chanting *ohm* as her gray curls hung over her laptop, which was perfectly balanced on her open palm. I closed my eye to rest it.

"Too bright?" she asked, flicking off the fluorescents.

The reduction of light sent a clear image of her to my brain. Only this time, her hair was in a bun and she wore a white hat shaped rather like an upside-down Chinese take-out box. A purple blemish on her forehead stood out as she glared at me with a scowl. Her foul disposition likely rose from the tight white band wrapped around her waist, which polished off her stark-white skirted uniform.

"Silence," she ordered me with a bark.

My eyes shot open. "What?"

"The lights," she said. "I figured they were too bright. Is this better?" Leaning over, she examined my face. Her gray curls fell toward me.

"I-I don't know," I babbled. My mind swam with the crossover of mixed signals. "I don't know what's going on."

There. I said it.

Out loud.

"It's okay," she said. "Quite normal for a brain injury. And let's not forget you're likely traumatized from the violence of the accident. You need to allow yourself time to heal and recover."

"I don't even remember the accident," I mumbled.

"That's part of your defense mechanism," she said. "It's how your mind is coping with the shock of it all."

I studied her face. "How do you know so much?"

"It's my area of specialization," she said. "I'm the ER trauma doctor, but I specialize in brain injury. The rewiring of the brain after being damaged fascinates me."

"Well, can you explain why I'm seeing things then?" I huffed. "Maybe tell me why my brain is racing faster than I can keep up with it, sending mathematical calculations through my skull to interpret every potential probability of any and every concept that erupts in my mind." I took a breath. "And why I should even care about all the trivial facts about every subject I ever studied in school." I grabbed my head. "I'm sorry. It's just maddening. I can't stop it."

"It's post-concussion symptoms," she said with a calm voice.

"Right. Like emotional outbursts, anxiety, and sleep disturbances," I rattled off. "I know. They told me about what to expect when I was discharged last time." I moved my eyes away from her. She was no different from the other 'experts'. Then I mumbled, "No. It's more than that. I'm different now."

She stepped closer. "How do you mean?"

"I see things," I said.

It felt awkward to say, but maybe she might have heard about this sort of thing before. I certainly couldn't be the only one. Well, besides Kaitlin.

Her head tipped as she listened.

"And I feel things," I added. "It's like a new sixth sense. Like I'm living within a dream I can't wake up from."

"Your brain is rewiring," she said. "It's finding new neurological pathways and strengthening itself. It will feel strange and unreal at times."

"And *haunting*?" I asked. "It's more than what you're saying. Please, just tell me what it is. If you know so much about this, then tell me what it could be."

She put her laptop down on the end of my bed, then ran her hands through her hair.

"It's too early to be sure," she started. "But it sounds very possible." Her eyes narrowed, studying me.

"What?" I pressed her.

"It's a condition where a traumatic brain injury patient suddenly has new ability. Of a higher level. A genius level, even. Like that of a learned scholar or a sage." She paused. "The brain is open in new ways, using information that was once suppressed."

"What do you mean?" My eyes widened as I stared, waiting for her to say more.

"Acquired savant syndrome."

∾

Acquired savant syndrome? The term rolled through my mind and shed light in every corner, illuminating the truth of my condition.

I'd heard the term 'savant' before, usually referring to a six-year-old master piano player or a brilliant deaf composer. But I never realized it was something that could occur at a random point in time, after a brain injury.

But I was certain she was right about her diagnosis. My brain had rewired in ways that exploded my thinking to levels that reached near paranormal. I had even looked right into Kaitlin's face that first day I woke up in the hospital, and she was in a different room.

Something was strange. And it was evolving quickly. My doctor said it was only the beginning, which rattled me even further. She said the brain could take weeks or even months to finish its healing, and I was still only on week one since the accident.

If my migraines subsided, they'd release me from the hospital by the end of the day. Once discharged, I'd research the hell out of acquired savant syndrome. And find out if Kaitlin had it, too. Although that answer screamed its own truth in my face, clear as day. She saw the woman at the tree. And she saw something, or felt something, at the front door of the Excited Ward, too. Something sinister.

"So where's your handsome boyfriend?" The nice nurse returned to check my vitals.

"He's not my..."

"Oh, right. He's not your boyfriend," she interrupted with a chuckle. "My bad. So how are you feeling?"

"I'm good," I answered quickly. "Feeling strong."

She narrowed her eyes. "You sound too convincing."

"No, really..." I hesitated, cringing at my overzealous response. I took it down a few notches. "I think the resting helped. I feel decent now. Like, the headache is much better."

"Are you sure?" She studied me as if she could read my true thoughts.

"Yes. I'm sure," I said, holding my eyes open to hide their natural desire to squint from the stabbing pain driving straight into my brain.

"Well, I'll get clearance from your doctor and will contact your mother to come for…" Her voice morphed into a mixture of instructions that then turned to liquid-like warning that oozed all over me.

I squeezed my eyes shut to block out the vision of her melting face. My migraine was taking on a new level of pain that was causing terrifying hallucinations. Even with my eyes closed, her face continued to drip as her words tormented me, poking at me with evil jabs.

"There's no one coming for you," her twisted voice cut at me. "You've been abandoned. Left here to rot."

My air sucked in with a gasp.

Her voice continued to harass me. "Wayward girl. Dancing with the devil. You're no good and you'll grow old here. Alone."

My eyes shot open with a gasp, and I stared in horror into my mother's face.

"You're dreaming, dear. Wake up." She rubbed my arm. "I'm here to take you home."

~

Settling into my own bed in my own room seemed like it should have felt like utopia, but all I could think about was getting in touch with Kaitlin. It had been at least three days since we were at the asylum, and I needed to talk to her.

My phone had been packed into a plastic hospital bag with my name and room number written on it with black Sharpie. Socks with rubbery skid-proof patterns and my brown jacket filled the bag, and made it impossible to find the phone. Finally, my prodding latched on and pulled it from the bag.

"No screen time, Grace," Mom called from the kitchen as if her extra-sensory perception had kicked in.

I fumbled for my charger, cursing at the evil dark depths of my unresponsive black screen. "Shit," I murmured, impatiently pressing the button to get it to turn on.

Finally, it glowed to life. As I scrambled to begin typing a message, Kaitlin's three dots bleeped into a full paragraph of text.

Wtf
Answer meeeeeeee
I've seen so much its driving me crazy
R u seeing it too
GRACE
GRACE
GRACE

I texted back as fast as I could.

Kaitlin
I'm home now
I need to talk to u

FaceTime lit up in two seconds flat.

"Holy shit," she squealed into the screen. "What the hell happened to you? Braden said you were a mess."

"He did?" My shame burned my face as her comment distracted me from my focus.

"No, not really, but I could just tell," she said. "You kind of freaked him out. What the hell happened?"

I rubbed my eyes. "I don't know. I had the craziest migraine. Like, I went blind from it. It was so scary." I shook my head. "I literally thought it was permanent. I've never been so scared in my life."

"That's insane," she said. "I swear, the same was nearly gonna happen to me. My headaches are disgusting. Like a gross feeling of someone in my head messing with it. It's like I'm losing my mind and someone is there, making it happen."

"Jesus, Kaitlin. That's creepy," I mumbled. "Sucks, because, unfortunately, I know exactly what you're talking about."

We stared at each other through our phones as if not knowing what to say or do next.

"Why didn't you visit?" I asked. "Braden came instead."

She paused. "I asked him to go in my place."

"Why?"

"I couldn't do it, Grace," she said. "I was too scared." She looked away for a moment. "Like, when I'm near you, it makes everything… more. Like more intense."

"What do you mean?" I pressed.

"Like the visions…and the headaches," she said. "When I'm near you, they're even worse. And when I heard you went to the hospital again, for blindness, it scared the shit out of me." She stared into the phone. "I don't know what's happening, Grace. I feel like I'm losing my mind."

"It's acquired savant syndrome," I stated. "My doctor told me all about it. It's a condition that happens sometimes after a brain injury. It's rare, but it's real."

"Acquired what?"

"Acquired savant syndrome," I repeated. "Like developing a superpower after a head injury heals and rewires, even stronger than before."

"So we're superheroes now?" She chuckled.

I smiled back. "Yeah. I think so."

"So what do we do now then?" she asked. "Fight crime? Take over the world?"

I wish I shared her levity on this. But honestly, she just had no idea what all this meant. She probably still thought we'd get better. I was starting to believe this *was* our better. And I needed to figure out what it all meant and how we were going to live with this new shadow hanging over us.

"I think we need to go back to the asylum," I stated with flat affect.

"What? Why?" Kaitlin's eyes widened in fear.

"I don't know," I mumbled. "It felt odd there. Too many strange things were happening. Don't you agree?"

"It was just a creepy place," she said. "Of course our imaginations were going to run away with us."

But it was more than that, and she knew it. It scared her.

"Don't you just want to see more of it?" I pressed. "I mean, it's better than anything we've ever discovered."

Kaitlin's hand flew to her eye. "Ahh," she cried out, dropping her phone onto her bed.

"Kaitlin?" I called. "Are you okay?"

My screen displayed a still-white image of her ceiling, but I could hear her rustling.

"I can't do screen time," she murmured. "It's hurting my eyes." Her voice trailed off, but then erupted in a crash of pain and fear. "Grace!"

I stared at the white ceiling image in my phone, straining to get a glimpse of her. "What is it, Kaitlin?" I yelled.

"The woman," she screamed. "I keep seeing the woman!"

"What woman? What's going on?" I shouted back.

"The one hanging from the tree," she cried. "And she's alive. She's... calling to me."

"Holy shit, Kaitlin! It's a dream! Shake it off!" And in that same instant, the feeling of a red-hot poker drove into my brain, causing me to hunch over in agony.

An image of the same girl shot through my mind. She stood at the top of concrete steps at the entryway to a brick building. Her heavy skirts and thick shawl swayed with her agitated movements as she shook her arm at me, twisting her face with strained effort. Her lips moved as her face contorted, trying to be heard, and she repeated the same word again and again until I finally heard her raspy voice.

My spine straightened and I sat up tall in my bed, eyes wide, searching for the source of the sound that resonated through my skull.

"Did you hear that, Kaitlin?" I whispered into my phone.

All I could detect was her quiet whimpering.

Then the girl's voice burst through my mind again, and I dropped my phone as she shouted, "Run!"

CHAPTER 9

The girl's command to run was clear as day but it somehow had the opposite effect. All I wanted to do was go back to her. I needed to return to the asylum and search for answers. There was something there calling to us. Like something or someone needing to communicate. And somehow, Kaitlin and I had the ability to hear it. And to see it.

We had to go back.

We had a new gift. The doctor plastered a fancy term on it, acquired savant syndrome, but I had a better term.

Medium.

That girl was reaching out to us, and we could see her. We actually heard her voice calling out to us.

Whatever it was, I needed to know more. And the only way to get more information was to go back to the condemned asylum.

The biggest hurdle would be convincing Kaitlin. She was terrified of the girl and every unusual sensation that ran through us when we thought of the institution. But I refused to be haunted by the visions. I needed to understand them. Figure out their message.

"Are you freakin' crazy?" she warbled through the phone.

I thought a good night's sleep would recharge her and bring back her adventurous curiosity. Her anxious tone and bulging eyes proved I was wrong about that.

"What? You don't think we should go back?" I pressed.

"No, I do think we should go back," she chided. "But we have to. I know. But you're crazy if you think we should go back without the guys."

I huffed in relief. She realized we had to return, too. That was a start. And she was willing to go. That was also a good thing. But she was stuck on the part where I suggested we go without the guys. And this was the part I felt strongly about.

Braden and Nick wouldn't understand. They'd only be a distraction, treating it like a circus. And I felt it deserved more respect than that. Kaitlin and I needed to go alone. To explore every inch of the place, without fooling around or vandalizing anything. I just felt like we needed to go in a different mindset this time.

I explained my thinking to Kaitlin, and she pushed back.

"It's not safe, Grace," she said. "We need them as our protection."

"We do not," I shot back at her. "We'll go during the day and obviously won't put ourselves in any dangerous situations. We just need to look around again, Kaitlin. On our own, so we can focus."

She rolled her eyes, acknowledging her acceptance of my plan, however much she didn't like it.

"When?" she asked with a flat tone.

I paused for a second, and then said, "Today."

Kaitlin was pissed, acting like going back to the asylum was the last thing she'd ever want to do. But, ironically, she pulled up in front of my house within minutes of our decision to go.

"I can't believe your mom let you take the car," I squealed, climbing in.

"Oh, shit! That reminds me." She grabbed her phone. "I need to put this on ghost-mode again, so she doesn't track me. She thinks I'm just hanging out with you and going to the mall." She updated her app, then put the car in gear. "Are we sure about this?"

I clicked my seat belt. "Yup. We don't have to stay for long. I just need to know if any of that shit was real. Like, if any of it happens again, then we know something big is going on. If not, then yeah, maybe it was all just our heads playing tricks on us."

Kaitlin shook her head and pulled out. "Maybe we won't even be able to find it again. Maybe it doesn't even exist."

"Whatever." I glanced out my window.

Her reluctance was annoying. It made no sense she wasn't just as frantic about this as I was. Sure, it was scary, but there was no way I could ignore this and pretend like it wasn't happening.

"I can't believe your mom let you out of the house." Her words broke my train of thought.

"She doesn't know." I huffed. "She's at work. Probably until late again."

It used to bother me that she worked so much, but now I saw it as a blessing. All she did was hover judgmentally anyway, always wondering where I was going, who I was with, and if I'd been partaking in the sins of today's youth. I just wanted her to stay as far away from me as possible.

I stared out the window as we drove along the orchard roads, wondering what might happen when we got there. The place was everything Kaitlin and I ever dreamed of as we spent all of our past summers searching for ancient cemeteries or trying to uncover creepy urban legends. The mystery of the burned-down orphanage was our favorite. The stone-foundation ruins and sections of the basement were all that remained of the orphanage and were believed to be haunted. We'd explored that site so many times, though, it wasn't even spooky anymore.

But now we had a true mystery. It held secrets that scratched at our minds, never allowing it to be forgotten. We should be resting, but somehow the pull of that place was stronger than anything else.

I glanced up, catching a glimpse of the water tower.

"There." I pointed. "Pull in down that road."

THE SHUTTERED WARD

Kaitlin took the turn hard, causing the tires to squeal beneath us. I swayed, pressing against my door as we took the sharp corner.

"Sorry," she said, fighting the pull in the steering wheel. "Didn't want to miss it."

My face pressed against my window, and I stared out past a group of mature evergreens that shielded an open field behind them. Black spike fencing hid behind the brush, and I caught sight of its ivy-covered gate. My mouth pressed to the side as I contemplated what the secluded area might be.

"I think the pull-off is just up ahead a bit," I said, craning my neck back for a final look at the hidden field.

"I see it," she said as a twitch jolted through her entire body. "I can't believe we're doing this. Have you looked this place up? It has some pretty disturbing stories about its patients. Like, the criminally insane."

I glanced at my phone. It was true. I'd done a bit of research on the asylum, and I was unsettled by what I'd found. Abusive conditions, unethical treatment methods, a clinical research lab, notorious inmates.

"Like the boy who killed his parents?" I said.

"Yes! I saw that too," she interjected.

"He stabbed his mother and put a hammer through his father's skull," I summarized. "But then, he had no memory of the event. Like it never happened."

"They had no idea how to treat him in the hospital," she added. "Like a criminal or like a mental patient."

"There were a lot of people like that," I said. "They were kept in the high-security ward. But then there were the people whose families had them sectioned against their will."

"And others who signed themselves in," Kaitlin chuckled as she turned the car down the narrow lane leading to the institution.

The sound of the tires crunching on the broken pavement filled the car as she moved slowly over it. She pulled to the side of the road near the sign we'd originally found. I stared at the stone monument and its original inscription, **Blackwood Insane Asylum**, and a chill of death ran through me.

"Ready?" Kaitlin asked.

I stared up the broken road toward the clearing where the grounds of the asylum stood. A dull ache throbbed behind my eyes as if to warn me from what I might see. I rubbed them for longer than necessary, attempting to wipe away any disturbing visions or images that might still linger from the last time we were there.

I blinked at Kaitlin, holding down the nausea that rose in my throat from the clamp on my gut.

"Ready," I replied.

～

I stumbled on the crumbling pavement as we walked toward the entrance to the grounds of the asylum. Thin streaks of gray clouds covered the sky, making the brightness of day easier on my eyes. Light and sound sensitivity were some of the most common symptoms of concussions, and I hadn't been passed over in those areas, or any of them for that matter. Fatigue, heightened emotions, and cognitive challenges like confusion and difficulty making decisions were several of the other symptoms I'd been warned of, but I fought back on those. My brain had always been one-hundred-percent reliable. I was a sharp, quick-thinker, and I refused to accept any less.

Still, I wasn't quite myself yet. The healing process was slow and frustrating. Any physical signs of the accident, like bruising or sore muscles, were gone. But my damn head was still foggy as if someone filled it with obstructive cotton.

"Do you think it's going to rain?" Kaitlin's voice jolted me.

Shading my eyes as I lifted my head, I noticed darker clouds moving in. I checked my weather app.

"It says forty-percent chance later, so we're good for now," I said. "I smell it in the air, though. It's coming."

"You smell the rain?" Kaitlin glanced over with raised eyebrows.

I slowed for a second under her scrutiny, realizing I'd never smelled the rain before. Or I'd never noticed, anyway. Right now, it was clear as day, but rain was coming.

"I don't know," I replied. "I think I've heard people say that before, and I kind of just noticed it myself."

"Well, let me know when it starts to get closer, so we can make a run for the car," she said with a chuckle.

We stepped out of the overgrown wooded area, and the clearing of the grounds opened up in front of us. The red brick buildings stood waiting for their visit, as if each one vied for our attention. And every single one had mine. I needed a full month at least to explore them, one by one.

But there was a pull that drew me back to the wards near the dining hall. The women's wards. Tom had described them to us as the Excited Ward, the Convulsing Ward, the Untidy Ward, and the Quiet Ward. I needed to see them again.

"Let's go this way." I pointed along the road that led to the wards. "I want to have a good look at those buildings."

Kaitlin slowed. "I forgot how creepy this place was," she mumbled. "And this time, with no sun, it's even creepier."

She was right. The last time we were here, the sun brought the place to life, reflecting bright rays off the old lead glass windows at the top floors of the buildings and shining bright orange hues off the red brick exterior of the wards. But now, everything was dull and gray.

We strolled along the broken pavement that must have once seen thousands of patients. I pictured them walking in head-down silence with stoic nurses at the front and back of the lines to keep order.

A flash of the hanging tree caught my eye. My eyes darted to Kaitlin as she took it in.

"Do you see anything?" I whispered.

"No." She shook her head. "Thank God." She turned away from it toward the row of wards along the outer edge of the grounds.

I tried to imagine what it would have been like to be confined to one of the wards. The gothic architecture was unsettling in its boarded-up, abandoned state, but even when alive and bustling, I couldn't picture their beauty. The buildings were ominous and foreboding. Prison-like.

"We need to explore that one." I gestured to the Excited Ward. It was the one in the middle of the others. The one that mesmerized us the last time we were there. Something about it pulled me closer.

"That's the freaky one," Kaitlin replied. "I'm not going near that one."

"We have to, Kaitlin," I pushed. "It's the one that matters. That's why it's freaky. Come on." I took her arm, pulling her along with me to the front of the ward.

She kept her gaze down, refusing to look directly at it. But I was determined to learn its secrets and I stared at its front entrance, daring it to open up to me.

Seven crumbling concrete steps led up to the boarded front door. Rolls of peeling white paint hung from the side pillars and crown moldings that framed the entryway. A crooked metal lamp, like one seen in an old medical examination room, hung from the overhang above the door. A large arched window high above kept watch through its array of small glass panes. I strained to see through the glass for a glimpse into the top floor of the building, but only the reflection of gray sky and branches from a nearby tree could be seen.

I moved up the front walkway toward the steps.

"Wait," Kaitlin said. "What are you doing?"

"I'm just gonna see if there's any weakness at the door. You know. To see if we can get in."

"Are you nuts?" she hissed.

I walked up the steps, minding my footing on the broken concrete, careful to not damage it any more. On the landing, I stepped closer to the door and put my hands on the plywood covering. Solid screws, positioned at regular intervals all around its perimeter, held it firm. I turned my attention to the side windows that framed the door, and I pressed on the boards that covered them. They, too, were sealed tight. I wished I'd brought a screwdriver or something I could wedge in behind them.

I turned back to Kaitlin. "They're boarded tight," I said.

She exhaled for miles and glanced back the way we'd come, likely hoping it was time to go.

"Follow me," I said as I hopped off the stairs and moved around to the side of the building. "Let's look for weaknesses around back."

Maybe there would be a loose board or a low window that hadn't been sealed well.

"The sign says 'Entry is prohibited. Danger. Police take notice,'" she said. "Have you not seen the signs?" She pointed to two different postings. "That one says cancer on it. Asbestos warning. That shit's dangerous."

"They have to post all those warnings," I said. "That way, the town's not liable if someone gets hurt. It's a 'proceed at your own risk' disclaimer, basically."

"Um, that's your la-la voice talking," Kaitlin grumbled. "You know, the one who says you're lost in your fantasy world. The one full of rainbows and unicorns. This is real, Grace. And it's dangerous."

I chuckled at her insult, but she was right in a way. Any time I tried to convince her to do something scary or devious, she said I used my 'la-la voice' to try to make it seem okay. And it was true—I was using it now.

I hurried to the rear of the building, my eyes widening at the immense size of the ward. It went farther back than I'd expected, and two separate wings moved out along the two sides, creating a U-shape at the back. Within the courtyard of the U were countless windows and low doors hiding in sunken stairwells to the basement.

I stared at Kaitlin in shock. Her wide eyes proved she was just as overwhelmed.

"Over there." A muffled voice caught my attention.

My head shot in the direction of a girl's voice from high above, and I scanned the top windows of the buildings. Then I moved my eyes to the inner corner of the U to a stairwell that moved down to a weathered basement door. The boarding looked rotted and broken.

I glanced up in the direction of the voice, but I saw nothing.

"Over there," I said to Kaitlin. "That door looks like a weakness."

CHAPTER 10

We crept toward the rotted basement door at the inner corner of the U-shape at the rear of the ward. I glanced once more to the windows above where I thought I'd heard the voice of a girl call to me. Logic told me it was my imagination or a trick of the wind, but my intuition nagged at my gut as if we were supposed to be here—to get inside the Excited Ward.

My heart rate quickened as my adrenaline surged through my veins. I'd always wanted to explore an abandoned place like this, only this one exceeded every expectation I ever had. The ruins of an insane asylum went far beyond anything I could have hoped for.

"Holy crap." I turned to Kaitlin as I approached the basement door. "The screws are rotted out. And the plywood is falling apart." I scanned around to be sure no one was watching, then stepped down the concrete stairs.

The metal railings on either side were rusted to near disintegration, and a pile of leaves and mud had accumulated at the landing below. My sneakers squished into the black muck as I kicked away some of the leaves that bunched up at the bottom of the damp, splintering board.

Kaitlin fearfully peered over her shoulder. "What are you going to do?"

Reaching my fingers behind the board, I tugged. A chunk of plywood came loose in my hands and fell to the ground. I gripped the side again and pulled more gently, jimmying the entire board from its housing.

"It's coming off," I whispered in astonishment as I gazed in behind the barrier. "Shit! I can see the metal door behind it."

I peeked around the jamb, searching for the doorknob, and saw only the round housing where the knob used to be. It had been broken off. When I pushed on the cold, rusted door, it pressed inward with stiff resistance.

"It's open," I squealed. "Come on. Squeeze through with me."

Pulling the plywood outward, I pressed behind it and pushed my weight against the metal door. It gave way enough for me to pry myself through, and I stumbled into the musty space within the lower floor of the building. I shot my eyes in every direction, searching for any sign of anyone or anything, but the space was silent.

"Hurry up," I called to Kaitlin. "Don't leave me in here alone."

Kaitlin bounced in place with indecisive nervous energy.

"Kaitlin," I pressed.

"Okay," she hissed through clenched teeth.

She squeezed her way in and stood against the doorframe, frozen. I stepped past her, pulled on the plywood to make it look like it hadn't been disturbed, then closed the metal door to the point just before it settled into its frame...just in case it decided to lock somehow...on its own.

Light entered the space through the loose sides of plywood boards that covered each window, but I still pulled out my phone to use its flashlight. I aimed my light beam in a steady motion across the entire room. Old metal file cabinets lined the side wall and taped boxes, blackened by mildew, were piled on top of them. A rusted bookcase keeled to one side from the weight of an old-fashioned typewriter and a film projector that still had two reels attached to it. More boxes labeled 'confidential' filled the shelves of the decrepit bookcase, and wooden clipboards were strewn all over.

"It's a storage room or something," I whispered.

Dusty beams of light shot across the room from the narrow seams at the windows, illuminating the peeling paint from the walls around us. Layer after layer, exposing assorted colors of past decades, rolled down the walls on every square inch. At the far side of the room, my eyes landed on a chipped white door with two rows of small-paned windows at the top, four on each row. It was slightly ajar, inviting us farther into the secrets of the ward.

"This is insane," Kaitlin whispered. "I can't believe all the stuff that's still in here."

"Same." I stepped closer to the white door.

"What are you doing?" Kaitlin froze.

"Exploring," I said. "Come on." I pulled the wooden door open wider, and it creaked on its rusted hinges. My shoulders lifted to my ears in an attempt to quiet its alarm.

I peered out into a long corridor with archways that spanned the width every few feet. Piping, wrapped with ripped cloth that hung like decaying bandages on a mummy, crossed overhead while large cardboard cans overflowing with trash lined the sides of the hall.

"Let's see if there's a way to get to the upper floors," I whispered. "There must be a stairwell at the end." I snuck out into the hallway, then tiptoed through the wide corridor. Doors leading to unknown areas, like boiler rooms or more storage, hid in every alcove begging to be opened, but my focus was on the upper floors and the stories they might hold for us.

Kaitlin followed close behind me, flinching at every ping or creak. "What's that?" she hissed.

"It's just the old pipes or the wind outside," I said.

"No, that." Slowing, she pointed to red splatters on the wall.

As we got closer with our lights, the splatters turned to swirls of spray-painted letters. We aimed our phones along the length of wall that led to a dark stairwell, revealing the full extent of the graffiti.

It read, "Help Us".

I sucked in a breath as I stared at the creepy faded words, reminding myself we weren't the only ones intrigued by this place.

"Shit. That's freaky." Kaitlin choked on her words.

"Don't worry," I said. "It's just from teenagers who broke in before us. It's old. Probably from before they boarded the place up, so…"

Kaitlin stared at the entryway to the stairwell, and I followed her gaze.

More red spray lettering jumped out at us as if in warning.

RUN!

～

The warning outlined in bold graffiti shot terror through my soul. The timing was cruel. I'd just mustered enough courage to climb the dark stairs to the first floor of the ward when I saw the word 'RUN'. Somehow, that one word held enough power to make me reconsider my plan to climb. Instead, I wanted to turn on my heels and follow its command in full flight.

But I fought my natural instinct to get out of the abandoned, condemned building, taking a moment to regain my composure.

"That scares the shit out of me. Not gonna lie." I turned to Kaitlin with a smirk.

She didn't smile back. She stood frozen in her spot with her head shaking back and forth as terror poured from her eyes. "I can't go up there," she murmured. "It's a warning, Grace. We need to listen to it."

"Kaitlin. It's graffiti," I sighed. "If it was blood or zombified patients coming after us, I'd probably feel differently. But this is just some old vandalism by drunk teenagers. Don't let it spook you."

"I just have a bad feeling," she said. "And you always say I should listen to my gut."

"Yeah, but that's not your gut," I added. "It's you being a puss…"

"Okay, okay, I get it," she blurted as I teased her.

I grabbed her hand, then tugged her onto the stairs with me. We climbed to the first landing. A large arched door led to the outside, but the blocked-out window proved it was boarded tight. We turned and went up the next set of stairs where another aged door with a metal handle and a small square window waited for us. It was as if it were ready to lead us into the first floor of the ward.

I glanced up the following flight of stairs, then noticed they were enclosed in tightly woven chain-link fencing. The cage-like feel sent shivers through me, and I wondered why they would fence in the passage through a stairwell. I pivoted toward the old, heavy wooden door, then reached for its handle.

With a bump from the side of my body, the door opened, sending a stagnant musk stink into our noses, making my lips itch. We stepped into the wide corridor, the vast length of it intimidating. Dusty light crept through any crevices left at the edges of the boarded-up windows. Just enough of it glowed at the far end of the hall to illuminate a lone object. A single beam of light cast upon it in its silent alcove of darkness.

"Holy crap," I whispered. "That looks like an old-fashioned wheelchair."

Water pooled on the broken tile floor, dripping from the sagging pipes above. Sounds of droplets splashing in shallow puddles echoed through the hall, blending with the sound of our heavy breathing.

"Let's go up to the next floor," Kaitlin said. "Maybe it's less gross."

We backed up into the stairwell again. At the top, I pulled the solid door shut to seal in, or block out, the decomposing sight of the building. Then we took a few steps up in the caged-in stairwell. As we climbed, I looked down between the fencing through the center shaft that led all the way to the basement. The fencing was likely a safety precaution in case someone fell over the railing. I poked my fingers into the small links, noticing the inability to gain traction to climb.

I blinked my eyes slowly in thought. As I opened them, an image flashed in front of me, causing me to jump back.

"What is it?" Kaitlin cried, sounding startled.

"It's a suicide cage," I said. "To stop people from jumping."

"How do you know that?" She gazed down the center of the stairwell into the darkness at the bottom.

I wasn't sure, actually. Maybe a movie or a book I once read. But clear as day, it was a suicide cage. Its one purpose was basic and unapologetic.

I shrugged, continuing to climb to the next floor of the Excited Ward. My heart pounded in my ears as I stepped toward a heavy door with a metal handle, identical to the one below it. I turned to Kaitlin. When she nodded, I pressed the handle down and pushed the door with my body. After some initial stubborn resistance, the door squeaked on its hinges, sending the sound of lost, screaming souls straight through us.

Kaitlin grabbed my arm. She squeezed her fingers deep until it felt like I would bleed. "Stop," she hissed. "It's too loud." And she reached for her ears to block the sound.

My nerve endings tingled all over as a shudder of fear quaked through me. "It's just the door hing…" But my words were cut short by a blast of wind that felt like a stampede of souls bursting past us to escape to their freedom. Some of the gusts seemed to move right through me, leaving me breathless.

I turned to Kaitlin, whose face had turned ghostly white, and she mumbled words on repeat.

"2352362352362," she whispered.

"What are you saying?" My voice choked in my throat as I heard the muffled numbers.

They were the same numbers that entered my mind back in the hospital. A string of taunting numerals that tormented me deep in my bones.

"Stop it," I growled through clenched teeth. "Be quiet," I snapped.

Pupils blown wide, she silenced her relentless chanting. But she reached for her ears again, then pressed her hands against them, body rocking. "I want to get out of here," she begged.

The numbers repeated in my mind like a digital ticker on the stock market. I squeezed my eyes shut to try to clear them out of my head. "Okay. Let's get out of here," I agreed.

We turned back toward the stairwell, panic-stricken, as a surge of flapping filled the caging from below, creating a mind-shattering barrage of clanging metal and thunderous pounding. A black blur swiped past Kaitlin's head and flew up the stairs. She swatted at is as another shot straight for my face and then twisted direction, bombing higher.

"Bats!" Kaitlin pushed against me as a whir of black clouds filled the stairwell and shivered with chaos all around us. "Millions," she screamed.

"Quick," I blasted. "Up the stairs."

I grabbed her and we raced higher to the next floor. But the bats were faster, swarming around us from every direction.

"In here!" I pushed the heavy door of the third floor open, swatting at the black frenzy, and we rushed through, slamming it behind us.

Panting into the decaying corridor, we bent and held our knees. As I caught my breath, I lifted my head, scanning our surroundings. Peeling paint hung from every wall and chunks of ceiling fell, dangling, from above. Light filled the hall through large, lead glass, too high up to require boarding.

The light was so bright, I squinted my eyes to narrow slits. And then, in the haze of my panic and the shadows of my closing lids, I saw her.

Although this time, she wasn't hanging from a tree.

She was waving for us to come closer.

∼

Her dark shawl covered her shoulders and ran down the sides of her floor-length skirt, filthy at the bottom hem from dragging endlessly along the dirty ground. A gray frock covered her as a top layer, and its torn pocket stole my attention. A black ink stain spread out on the fabric. It resembled a huge, creepy spider, making my hair stand on end.

As if she knew us, her expression brightened, and she waved for us to come closer.

Kaitlin grabbed my arm. "A ghost."

"No," I replied with certainty. "She's real." I took a few steps closer, hearing my feet crunch on chunks of fallen plaster from the ceiling.

Keeping my eyes on her, I inched closer, pulling Kaitlin along with me.

Kaitlin resisted, her feet firm in one spot. "I'm not going any closer. Who the fuck is she?"

I stared at the girl as feelings of familiarity flooded me. It was like a dream or more deja vu. The expression in her eyes proved she knew us. And somehow, it felt like I knew her, too, like a long-lost friend I hadn't seen for years.

"It's in our heads, Kaitlin," I whispered. "Our sixth sense. The mystery of this place is messing with our brains, flashing images of something we've seen somewhere else. I don't know. It's the only explanation."

She refused to take a step closer. "No. You said it yourself. She's real." Her voice cracked.

I stared at the vision of the girl and she moved out of view behind an arch in the hall. "I mean she's real, like in our minds." I pulled gently on her arm. "Please. I just want to see what's down the hall. Please."

"Grace, I'm scared."

"Me too." I tugged at her again. "But you feel it, too I know you do. We can't turn back now."

She inched her feet along the floor, scuffing through the dusty debris. Relief coursed through my veins as Kaitlin joined me again, and I turned my full attention to the archway.

We walked through the hall passing several doors, one after another, along both sides. Each door had a small, cross-shaped window in the center. My eyes darted to the windows of each door as I attempted to see into one, but the fogged glass, covered from years of soot, made it impossible. I resisted my temptation to stop and open one for fear of losing my connection with the girl up ahead of us. She'd led us this far, and I had to keep my focus on the exact location where she stepped out of sight.

One more archway and another set of doors with cross-shaped windows, and we moved closer to the exact location where the girl had been. I studied the floor for markings of her footsteps or drag marks from her long skirt, hoping to follow her trail. Instead, my ears perked up in response to a sound coming from just beyond the arch.

I sucked my breath in and held it, listening for any more sounds. Kaitlin froze next to me and she stared, waiting to see what I would do next.

I leaned forward to see past the side of the archway. A door was nestled into the corner, hidden by the architecture. My eyes widened as I stared at Kaitlin. The end of the hall was just ahead with an alcove to the right—likely another stairwell. Taking a deep breath, I noticed the door was slightly ajar. I swallowed hard.

The door was different from the others. It didn't have a small, cross-shaped window but instead had a full-sized glazed one that let the light in but was impossible to see through. Chipped, faded lettering clung to the glass and read, 'Staff Only'. I reached for the brass doorknob, then pushed it farther open.

I searched the room for the girl, but she was nowhere to be seen. Vanished into thin air.

"She's gone," I whispered to Kaitlin as she inched along behind me.

"You sound disappointed," she murmured as she checked all around.

"It's just weird," I said as I stepped into the room.

An aged wooden desk sat in the middle with an old, bent-framed metal fan perched at the edge. A swivel chair with wheels lay on its side by the desk, broken. Another wooden chair sat in front of the desk, as if waiting to be disciplined by an angry principal.

"It's an office," I said. "Like, for the psychiatrist, maybe. I bet the patients would sit there, and the shrink would try to figure out why they were crazy."

"That sucks," Kaitlin mumbled. "How would anyone *not* seem crazy in here? They'd lose their minds just from being held hostage. And whatever went on in here would only make them crazier."

"And how do you convince someone you're not insane, when they already believe you are?" I stepped around the desk to the windows, scanning outside along the back of the building. "And there's nothing out there. Just woods. Total isolation." A feeling of terror brewed in my gut. "I'd go crazy if I ever got trapped in here."

I backed away from the windows toward Kaitlin, noticing yellowed papers sticking out from the top drawer of the desk. My feet carried me to it in two swift steps, and I jimmied the drawer open. It stuck on its tracks after opening a few inches, and I yanked harder until it came farther out.

Old, moldy notepads with 'Blackwood' written on top were strewn around the drawer amongst broken pencils. At the side of the drawer was a small cracked-leather booklet. I pulled it out to examine it.

"What is that?" Kaitlin stepped closer.

"I don't know." I opened the binder and found a few loose sheets within—sheets from the notepads, only these ones had writing on them.

I took the one from the top, studying the nearly illegible script. It had a name at the top. And a date. The middle had a short sentence, like orders. Then a smear of a signature at the bottom.

"It looks like an old-fashioned prescription," I said as I stared at it more closely, trying to read the scrawl. "Em…Emma Gr…Emma Grangley," I said, sounding out the possible letters. "It's written for someone named Emma, I think." I tried to read the middle part. "Unruly. Defiant. Uncontrollable. Immediate action, it says. Orb…orbital." I faltered on my pronunciation. "Orbital lob…lob-something. I can't read it."

"Orbital lobotomy," Kaitlin whispered, horrified. "It's a prescription for a freakin' lobotomy, Grace!"

I dropped the book and the paper like they were venomous. My vision went blurry as the room closed in on me. Every part of my body started to sweat as my breath moved in and out of me faster than I could control.

A full-blown panic attack.

"Help me!" The words exploded in my brain, causing me to jump.

"What is it, Grace?" Kaitlin searched me wildly.

Then she heard it, too

"Help me," the voice said, breaking all around us, and we flew for the door to escape.

CHAPTER 11

Escaping from the Excited Ward was our primary focus as terror ripped through our souls. The harrowing sound of Emma Grangley calling for our help rattled me to my core. I was sure it was her. There was no doubt in my mind. She needed us to save her. But we were powerless.

Sadness saturated me as I realized I couldn't help her. It was too late. The weight of grief bore down on my shoulders, making them slump. I pictured her face in my mind. Her laughter filled my memories, and her devious, whimsical nature made me smile. She was a free spirit, pushing back on the rigid rules of society. But society pushed back and punished her.

How did I know that?

My focus returned with a loud-pitched hum.

"This way," Kaitlin screamed. "Grace, come on!" She yanked me out of the office toward the stairwell beside it.

Blinking, I responded to the adrenaline that shot through my veins. Pure terror surged in my chest, and I ran with Kaitlin. We flew down the caged stairwell to the floor below.

"To the basement," she yelled. "Hurry!"

We raced down more steps, but then the stairwell was blocked off by metal fencing secured by padlocks and chains.

"We'll have to go through there." I pointed to the door that led into the first-floor wing. "If we run to the other end, we'll find the stairwell we originally came up through."

We kicked at the door, trying to push it open. A surge of cold air burst at our backs, forcing us through the opening. We hurried along the dimly-lit corridor, illuminated only by the light that poked through the tops of the boarded windows. Our feet splashed through puddles as the sound of dripping water echoed louder than physically possible—our senses piqued to overload.

Avoiding areas of pooled water, we skirted along the sides of the dilapidated hallway, passing canisters of debris and piles of broken furniture. I hopped over a heap of rotted burlap bags, then missed my landing, slipping across slimy mold on the floor. Grabbing the handle of a door for stability, I regained my balance only to fall again as it swung open. I held the handle to keep myself from face-planting and then stood, staring into a laboratory of some kind.

"Don't stop," Kaitlin cried as she continued down the hall as fast as she could.

But I couldn't pull my eyes away from the room no matter how hard I tried. Stainless-steel machines lined the walls, with round glass gauges all over the fronts and wires hanging from the sides. An oversized metal tub filled the center of the room. Water overflowed from the basin as drops from the ceiling splashed into it. A headboard of temperature gauges and other implements stood over the tub while long straps hung from the sides. Metal fasteners at the ends of the restraints, rusting in the wetness on the floor, created red streaks on the tile.

I stepped back in horror. "What the hell?" My voice echoed in the room, and I turned on my heels. I ran to catch up to Kaitlin who was already at the end of the hall.

"Hurry up," she shouted. "Grace!" Her voice cracked in terror.

I barreled through the corridor, splashing in the puddles, not caring about what I might disrupt or how I might get soaked. I just needed to get out of there. Immediately.

I crashed into an old, broken wheelchair, stumbling around its rattling, rotting carcass. With every attempt to break myself away from it, it seemed to be in my way more. I finally kicked it across the floor and ran to Kaitlin.

She pulled the door open, and we flew into the stairwell. Taking two or three steps at a time, we barreled down toward the basement. The red spray paint graffiti welcomed us back and reminded us again. "RUN."

And we did.

We ran as fast as we could toward the storage room we'd originally entered through. The white door with eight small window panes remained open, waiting for us and we wasted no time accepting its invitation.

Bombing past the boxes, file cabinets, and outdated office supplies, we ran for the exit door to the courtyard, to our freedom. I yanked the heavy door open, then pushed on the rotted board that secured it from the outside.

Only this time, the board wouldn't budge.

It was sealed tight on all sides.

I kicked at it as Kaitlin's voice filled the back of my mind with her terrified screams.

"Open it!" She shoved my shoulders, trying to push past me.

The sound of my frantic breathing drowned out all other noise as I focused on the rigid board that once hung broken in its mount—now solid in its housing.

There was no way out.

We were trapped.

∽

I kicked at the door until pain in my legs and feet stopped me. Bending to lean on my knees, I panted from the exertion. Kaitlin's eyes bulged out of her head as she stared at me, waiting for a solution.

"How the hell is it boarded up?" I struggled to catch my breath. "It makes no sense."

Kaitlin looked back toward the storage room door and then at me. "I need to get out of here, Grace. What if that girl comes back? I don't want to see her again. Please." Her voice cracked like she was about to cry.

"Close the door," I said. "We can barricade it." I pulled a chair out of a pile of office junk.

"Like that will stop her," she groaned.

"Well, it's better than nothing." I nudged her to take the chair as I searched for other things that could block the door. "I'm calling for help." I reached in my pocket for my phone.

"Wait. Who?" she snapped. "My mother will kill me if she knows I came here. I'm sorry, but she told me not to hang out with you right now."

My gaze shot to her. "What? Why?"

She shook her head as she jammed the chair under the doorknob. "She thinks you're unstable."

I stopped what I was doing, shocked. "Unstable?"

She shrugged, digging for more things to block the door. "Your mom called her. Told her you were freaking out with weird visions and shit. My mom's scared of you now, basically."

Anger surged through me, causing my face to burn red. It was as if my mother were enjoying this. She was always looking for anything sinister in me. Something deviant. And now she finally had it. Sure, it was head trauma caused by a car accident, but if she wanted to make it sound like I was possessed, then fine.

"I seriously hate her," I mumbled.

"You shouldn't say that," Kaitlin whispered.

"No, Kaitlin. This time I can," I grumbled. "This is the last straw. She doesn't have my back and never has. She always says I'm too much like my father, and I think that's been eating away at her all these years."

A banging sound came clanging along the pipes overhead.

"Shit. What's that?" Kaitlin whimpered.

In two seconds flat, I had my phone ready and called Braden.

Before he could finish saying 'hello,' I interrupted him with the details of our predicament without taking a moment for a breath. First the breaking in, then the vision of the girl showing us to the doctor's office, the ocular lobotomy, the overflowing tub...

"How the hell are you trapped?" His voice blasted through the phone at me. "If you came in through the door, you should be able to leave through it."

"No, it's impossible," I pleaded. "It's like someone screwed it shut while we were in here. Please! You have to come. Bring a screwdriver or a crowbar. Anything! Just get us out of here."

"I'm on my way," he assured me. "How will I know where to find you?"

"We're in the back of the Excited Ward," I explained. "Directly across from the dining hall. We're at the door at the far right in the courtyard at the back of the building."

No response. Silence sat heavily in my ear.

"Braden? Are you there?" I asked.

Nothing. Except for the heartbeat pounding in my ears.

"Is he gone?" Kaitlin gasped.

I swallowed hard. "Yes." I tried calling again, and it rang without an answer. I glanced around the room, then checked the charge on my phone. "I think he heard enough. He's coming."

With a nod, she came over to stand next to me. Her shoulder touched mine as she pressed in close, surveying the room for any spooks or oddities.

"What percent are you at?" I asked.

"Fifty."

"Okay, that's good. I'm at forty-eight," I said. "So, let's conserve our batteries and just use one flashlight at a time." I checked the time. "It's almost five o'clock. It'll be getting dark in a couple of hours. We'll need them if we're still here then."

"We better not still be here," Kaitlin snapped.

"We won't be. Don't worry." I glanced at the exit door, hoping it would miraculously burst open and Braden would charge in to rescue us. Cringe-worthy, I knew. But I would have done anything for that knight-in-shining-armor moment right now.

I slid down the wall until I squatted on the floor. Kaitlin lowered herself down with me. My face itched, and I scrunched my nose against the mold and dust that tickled at it. Shivers quaked from Kaitlin's body, passing on to mine and causing my nerves to compound into shudders.

I thought about how we'd get out of there. I could pile boxes and try to shimmy out one of the windows, but they were boarded solid. I'd wait a bit first to see if Braden came.

It was interesting that my first, and only, call was to Braden. I hadn't realized how much I relied on his friendship. He was the one I could count on who was always there to pick me up. I thought back to high school, remembering his cracking voice and acne. Even though he'd grown to be the tallest and most athletic of the boys, I somehow still saw him in that same light, as an awkward teen.

Plus, there was no one else to call. Anyone else would have no idea where to find us or would think we were nuts. If worse came to worst, I'd have to call my mother, and that was the absolute last thing I'd ever do. I'd rather break a window first and risk a patchwork of stitches along my arms. I supposed the police would be a final option as well. But deep down, I knew Braden was on his way.

I scanned the room, examining the contents.

"Don't even think about leaving this room," Kaitlin hissed. "I swear, I'm not stepping foot out there again. Ever."

I smirked and nodded in full agreement. "No, I'm just looking at all the crap in here. It's like they planned on moving it all out at some point and then just gave up. They walked away from it one day and never came back. Just sealed it up instead." I pushed myself to standing. "I'm dying to look in one of those boxes."

"Confidential," Kaitlin read aloud.

"Yeah, I'd say that label has expired," I said, moving toward the rickety file cabinets. "Help me get these down." I reached up, then pulled on a stack of heavy boxes.

The box on top wobbled as I wiggled the bottom one out to the edge of the cabinet. Just as the top box started to fall, Kaitlin grabbed on to it and lowered it to the floor. I set the other box next to it, then kicked it over to our safe spot by the wall. Kaitlin followed me, sliding her box as well.

We lowered ourselves down the wall again to squatting and stared at the boxes. The brown cardboard of my box was stained and worn from the years, but still held strong with its sturdy construction. Kaitlin's box was newer with red lettering along the sides for labeling. I pulled the lid off mine.

Two stacks of papers filled the interior. I flipped through the top pages and examined the handwritten papers, all in old-world black ink cursive, each sheet with the same heading, **MEDICAL HISTORY**. 'Name' and 'Age-at-committal' were on the top lines, followed by 'Place of birth' and 'Date' on the next lines. Then sections for 'Physical descriptions' and more spaces for 'Current condition' and 'Particulars of committal'. A line at the bottom held the signature of the medical examiner.

Kaitlin gazed wide-eyed at the old documents, then flipped the lid off her own box. She rubbed her hand across the tops of file folders and pulled one out. The papers inside were mostly completed by typewriter with the only handwriting being signatures and any attached prescriptions for Prozac. She turned her attention to my older records.

I leafed through the documents, hundreds or even thousands of identical forms, and gasped at the sheer volume of committed patients from the late 1800s and early 1900s. Conditions listed in the descriptions included things like mortified pride, disappointed expectations, melancholia, and moral insanity. Recommendations like restraints, hydrotherapy, insulin coma, and seclusion were listed just above the final signature.

I frowned at the power the medical doctors had over these women. Women who were probably perfectly sane but had pushed against a system that suppressed them. I couldn't get my head around the mistreatment and imprisonment of these unfortunate people. It wouldn't have taken long for them to become truly insane within these unforgiving walls.

Tears pooled in my lower lids. Kaitlin shook her head with similar disgust. Then my eye caught on the perfectly scrawled name at the top of the page that had just fallen through my fingers.

Emma Grangley.

～

Gasping, I pulled Emma's form out from all the others. Straining to read the streaked black ink that filled the document, I made out that she was committed at seventeen on '9 June 1919'. She presented as 'stubborn' and 'agitated,' and the section that listed 'particulars' said 'mortified pride' and 'uncontrolled passion'.

"Oh my God," I murmured at Kaitlin as I smacked my hand over my mouth.

"What does it mean?" She scrunched her eyes, trying to decode the messy ink scrawl.

"She was probably raped or something," I said. "Mortified pride must mean she was traumatized in some way, like violated. And any girl who was sexually active back then, even if it was against their will, would have been seen as a whore, so 'uncontrolled passion' would fit that description."

Kaitlin grimaced in revolt. "So they sent her to an insane asylum?"

"Probably to remove the shame from her family," I guessed. "Back then, rape would have brought disgrace to the family name. So sending her away—out of sight, out of mind—was their solution."

I pressed my lips together in tight judgment. It was a society run by men. Of course the women would suffer under their misguided rulings.

"What about 'stubborn' and 'agitated'?" Kaitlin pointed to the written description.

"I guess it's their way of saying she resisted her incarceration like a badass and fought when she realized she was trapped." Sickening anxiety rushed through my veins.

We were trapped here, too. I hoped not for long, but the feeling of being held against my own free will caused a panicked frenzy within me. Like a caged animal, I felt the angst to pounce and attack anything that threatened me. 'Stubborn' and 'agitated,' they called it.

My eyes trailed down Emma's medical form. A health survey listed her heart as 'sound,' lungs 'sound,' and genital health 'good'. I paused, feeling her violation as her captors examined her after she'd already been traumatized in that area. Sickness rose in my stomach, sending acid up into my mouth.

A box at the bottom of the document listed 'Prescriptives,' and this section was filled with a variety of recommendations for treatment. Restraints was the first item listed. Followed by isolation.

"What the hell?" I choked. "She didn't want to be here. She knew she didn't belong. So she fought, and all they did was restrain her and imprison her in solitary confinement."

"That's wrong on so many levels." Kaitlin shook her head. "It's obvious just by looking at this one paper she was responding like a normal person who was being held prisoner for no reason."

I studied the next lines of treatment, piecing together the old language and blotched ink.

"Ice-water therapy?" I said out loud. "What the hell is that?"

I thought back to the strange metal tub I'd seen on the first floor, then knew exactly what it meant. Submerged into icy water to shock her into compliance. My mouth quivered as tears pooled in my eyes again.

"I can't believe this," Kaitlin whispered.

"Me neither." The page shook in my trembling hand. I was afraid to keep reading.

Somehow, Emma had made herself known to us. Maybe we'd seen her in an old photograph in the town library or in a history book in school. Maybe our head injuries and this location had triggered the memory. Either way, we'd seen her on the floor above—at the same time. My eyes shot wide as I thought of our first vision of her, hanging from the tree.

I scanned the document, studying the following treatments.

"Seizure therapy," I stated with venom in my tone. "What the fuck is that?" My anger oozed from every syllable.

"Remember when Tom showed us the wards?" Kaitlin said. "He called this one the Excited Ward, but the others were the Untidy Ward, the Quiet Ward, and the Convulsing Ward. I bet they sent her to the Convulsing Ward."

My head shook. Of course they did. They were trying to subdue her by whatever means possible. Each treatment became more extreme than the previous, until they reached their desired result —compliance.

"I've heard of shock treatment," I said. "Maybe they used it to cause seizures. Probably hoping to force the devil out of the patients that way. Dumbasses."

My head turned to the sound of tires crunching on gravel.

"Shit! Someone's out there," I screamed and jumped up.

Braden's voice called from outside, "Grace! Kaitlin!" Oh my God, the relief that ran through me was unreal. I could breathe again.

Kaitlin ran to the door, frantically pounding on it. "We're in here," she screeched as if her life depended on it

Emma's paper shook in my hand, and I folded it to take with me. Just as I made the first crease, the words of her final treatment orders jumped out at me. My heart plummeted, causing dizziness. I staggered and leaned against the wall, struggling to draw a full breath.

I stared at the words on the page in horror as they confirmed what we had seen on the notes in the doctor's office.

'Orbital lobotomy'.

CHAPTER 12

Flying into Braden's chest and burying my face in it was embarrassing to me now. But the sight of him coming through the plywood barricade, between the shuttered ward and my freedom, burst such joy through me that I couldn't stop myself from racing to him. Braden delivered my freedom to me, and I didn't know what to do with my immense gratitude. I just stared at him every chance I got, absorbing all of his features.

I clambered alongside him, pushing out through the boarded-up door in case it somehow sealed itself back up again. My twitching muscles proved my belief that anything was possible at that point.

Once outside the ward, the exploded pieces of my mind settled into a more rational balance. I pulled the scattered bits of information together into something that made sense.

Braden. Nick. A truck with a 'Maintenance' sign on the side. And Tom.

Then the questions erupted.

"What the hell happened?" I asked, staring at Tom—a power drill hanging from his hand.

"I didn't know you were in there," Tom pleaded. "I saw the board had fallen away, so I fixed it." He shook his head. "If I'd known you were in there…"

"It's not Tom's fault," Braden interrupted. "It's nobody's fault." He turned his gaze to me, lips pressed together. "It was dangerous to come here. Alone." He glared at me.

I dropped my eyes from his. He was right. So many things could have gone wrong. And they had.

"Neighbors say they hear screaming from this place at night," Tom added. "You just don't know what goes on in there. It could be dangerous."

"Screaming?" Kaitlin squeaked.

Tom nodded. "They say it could just be the wind. But sometimes, they wonder if it's the remains of the screams that used to fill these halls and echo through the trees."

I glanced at the bolted door and then up to the higher windows. Light reflected off the lead glass, creating ghostly shapes and subtle motion. I pulled my eyes away for fear of seeing something real.

He added, "Some say it comes from the wards. Others think it comes from the lost cemetery. Nobody knows for sure."

"Wait," I interjected. "Lost cemetery?"

Could it be the cemetery Kaitlin and I had been searching for?

"Yup." Tom nodded. "The patients were buried there unceremoniously. The gravestones didn't even have their names on them. Just small cement markers with the patient numbers engraved on the tops. A real shame." He glanced up at the Excited Ward. "Some volunteers placed lovely granite name plaques there a few years ago, though. A decent gesture to offer the forgotten souls some dignity. Better late than never."

A whimper crept out of Kaitlin. "Can we just go home?"

"Yup." Braden wrapped his arm around my quaking shoulders, then moved with me away from the ward. Nick and Kaitlin followed as Tom climbed into his truck.

"Just don't try anything like that again," Tom said to us with a stern tone. "Someone could get hurt." He passed another business card to Braden. "Call me if you want any more info on the place. No need to

THE SHUTTERED WARD

go breaking in." He glanced at me with a side eye. And then he pulled the truck away and drove around the building out of sight.

As we walked toward the front of the ward, I stared at each of its boarded windows. Its locked secrets. Its mystery.

I needed to go back in.

Tom's warnings made no difference. My curiosity had grown into an obsession, and I cursed at myself for not spending more time exploring inside. There were more rooms. More secrets that called to me. And I had to investigate and understand them better. It made no sense, but I just had to get back inside.

The urge was overwhelming, and I pulled away from Braden's hold.

I raced to the front entry of the ward and stood at the base of the cement stairs, gazing up toward the blocked door. A heavy sadness weighted down on my shoulders. It filled my neck, and my arms drooped from the burden. It was the same feeling that overpowered me the first time I stood in front of this ward. I knew Kaitlin had felt it that time, too.

She stared at me as if I had lost my mind.

"We're leaving," she called.

"I can't," I stated.

I had no idea why I needed to go back in there. The pull was powerful, like the ward was calling to me, begging me to come back in. Somehow, I couldn't resist its demand.

It was like it controlled me. Owned me.

I stepped onto the first crumbling stair.

Kaitlin yelled, "Stop!"

I took a second step. Then leaped up several more and planted my feet on the landing. In a swift effort, I pressed my fingers around the boards that sealed the entry. I pulled, searching for weaknesses. Anywhere there might be some give.

My focus was sharp. It held one purpose—gaining reentry into the Excited Ward.

My fingernails broke, splinters slicing into my nail beds. I kicked at the bottom of the boards, trying to loosen their hold.

Then my shoulder pulled back. Resisting, I fought to get back to my mission.

"Grace. Stop." Braden's voice pressed into my spiraling mind. "Stop." He pulled on me again. "What are you doing?"

The confusion in his voice pulled my attention away from the door, and I studied his concerned face. His eyes examined mine like he was searching for me, but I wasn't there. I returned to the door, feeling its pull for me to continue my efforts at gaining entry. My mind ran frantic again with the pursuit.

But Braden continued to pull on me. This time, with more force.

"What the fuck, Grace?" he seethed into my ear.

He lifted me off my feet, then carried me down the steps. My first instinct was to fight him. To resist with all my efforts. He was trying to stop me from the one thing that mattered. He was the enemy.

I squirmed and kicked, yanking my shoulders to release from his grasp. But he held firm, determined to remove me from the area.

Then, I stopped resisting. Collapsing against Braden, I noted the shock in all of their eyes. Even Kaitlin. Her jaw hung open.

Something happened to me. It was like I'd lost my sanity for a moment. And it scared me.

It was the ward.

The ward messed with my head. It made me crave it like a junkie, and it was all I could think about. Like insidious poison, it crept through me. Haunting me with visions of that girl. Emma. Tormenting me with its secrets. Empty rooms full of secrets.

It wanted something from me.

It needed something from me.

And it had a firm hold.

I needed to fight…

To keep my sanity.

∾

Humiliation washed over me as I kept a close eye on Braden's car in my side mirror. He insisted on following us home, probably to be sure

I didn't decide to turn around and go back. Kaitlin drove toward my house in silence. Her tense jaw said enough.

She turned the car onto my street and exhaled, releasing the breath she'd been holding since leaving the asylum.

"I felt it, too," she whispered.

"What?" I whipped my head to the side.

"I'm sorry I didn't say anything sooner," she said. "I was too scared." She parked the car in front of my house, then set her full attention to me. "It just freaked me out to see you react like that when it was exactly what I wanted to do, too. Grace..." She hesitated. "I want to go back inside, too. Why is that?" Her voice cracked.

I twisted in my seat toward her, blinking my eyes before they bugged out of my head.

"Kaitlin, there's something there. It's like it needs us to find it." I watched Braden's car pull in behind us and spoke faster. "I'm scared. But I feel like we need to go back."

"Me too," she agreed. "I don't want to feel this way, though. I just wish this would stop."

"But the cemetery," I added. "It's there somewhere. Don't you at least want to find that?"

She nodded her head.

Then my door flew open, and I jumped a mile.

"Come on." Braden reached for my arm. "Time to get inside to rest. You keep forgetting you're concussed, and you're acting like everything's fine. You need to heal, Grace. You, too, Kaitlin." His voice reprimanded me like a slap in the face. "You'll cause permanent damage if you don't give yourself time to recover. I mean it."

I pulled my arm away from him. "You sound like my dad."

The comment held sick irony since I had no memory of my dad's voice, and it only added to my annoyance.

"I don't care," he huffed. "I'm serious, Grace. This has gone too far. You just need to chill. Don't go back there again. Not until you're healed." He paused. "I'd prefer you never go back actually."

"I have to go back," I mumbled as I climbed out of the car.

He gripped the side of the door until his knuckles turned white.

His lips quivered as if trying to hold his next words in, but then they escaped.

"I'll tell your mother," he stated with averted eyes.

I shoved him out of my way and stomped onto my front lawn, mumbling under my breath.

"Don't you dare, Braden," I hissed. "Or we're done."

His shoulders sank like I'd knocked the wind out of him. He turned back toward his car where Nick sat. Nick rolled his eyes.

My mind jumped back to Kaitlin and everything she just told me, and my heart rate quadrupled. I just wanted time to talk with her. To figure out exactly what we were feeling. And what was happening to us.

I watched Braden shift his weight from one side to the other, like he didn't know what to do next.

"Fine," I said, suddenly feeling bad for him. "We'll rest. We'll take a break. Happy?"

"Yes," he replied. "I'll check on you later."

I dropped my head back and groaned.

And with that, he dropped into his car and peeled away, scattering gravel out from his tires.

Kaitlin turned to me, baring her teeth. "He's pissed."

"Yeah, I know." I followed his car with my eyes until it was out of sight. "Wanna go back?"

Her face paled, and she studied the car keys in her hand.

Then my front door smashed open.

"Grace Frances!" My mother's voice pierced through my heart.

Kaitlin chuckled at the sound of my full name flying from my mother's lips. She knew this meant I was in deep shit.

"Where the hell have you been?" Mom shouted. "Get into this house, right now."

We walked across the lawn toward the front porch. I looked back at the driveway, confused. Her car must have been parked in the garage. I'd assumed she wasn't home, and the shock of her presence sent a sour taste into my mouth.

Her hand lifted, stopping Kaitlin in her tracks. "Sorry, Kaitlin. It's time for you to go home. Grace needs to rest."

My blood boiled. Did she think I was an infant?

"Mom, it's fine," I protested. "Kaitlin can stay." Anger seethed through me at my mother's attempt to separate the two of us. "No," I shot back, holding my ground.

But her face clamped into a tight scowl. Her lips pressed into a thin line as her eyes narrowed to slits. Anger reddened her face, causing a dark blotch to appear on her forehead. It looked like it throbbed from the pressure of her rage. It turned deep purple, like a port-wine stain.

I hardly recognized her. Her face took on the appearance of someone different. Horrified, I gaped.

I turned to Kaitlin to clear my vision. As soon as I saw her similar reaction to my mother's transformation, my stomach churned.

Kaitlin's head shook as she stepped away.

I bent over and held my knees. Then the retching came. I puked right onto the slate walkway, sending splatters everywhere.

I spat into the grass, raising my head. My mother's face had returned to normal as she jumped toward me to help.

"I've got her," she said to Kaitlin. "You head home now." She waved her hand toward Kaitlin's car.

And then she led me into the house against every screaming nerve in my body.

~

After I stumbled into the house, I went straight for the bathroom to brush my teeth. The earlier trembling from my anger had now turned to quaking shudders. My shoulders jolted in spasms as I stared at my reflection in the mirror.

Dark circles had formed under my eyes, beyond the natural shadow from my flaking mascara. Staring at the golden tones in the blue of my irises, I rubbed under each eye to try to improve the situation, then ran my fingers through my hair. I was a mess. But mostly on the inside.

"Are you okay in there?" Mom's voice scratched through the door, making me jump.

"I'll be out in a sec," I mumbled.

If I could, I'd stay in the bathroom for the rest of the night if that meant I didn't have to see her again. It sucked I felt that way about my own mother, but honestly, she forced it. She acted more like a warden than a mom. Her emotional detachment had been so painful my whole adolescence, and now it was over. I was grown. She'd missed it.

And I wasn't about to let her get involved at this point.

My mind jumped to Kaitlin. It was critical we communicated immediately. We had so much to talk about. And with Mom as my roadblock, I needed to smooth things over and convince her I was okay.

Was I?

Nope.

Not at all.

But she couldn't help me, so there was no need to involve her.

I cracked the bathroom door open and stepped out. She waited on the couch in the living room.

"Feeling better?" she asked.

"Yes. I think I just got a little dizzy," I said, rubbing my head. "I'm just going to lie down and rest."

"Just a minute," she said. "I want to talk to you. Sit." She pointed to the armchair across from her. "You are not taking your recovery seriously, and we need to discuss your plan for healing."

I pressed my eyes shut and rubbed them, then sat in the chair. I glanced at Mom, then focused into the dining room to avoid her glare. Without warning, my body twitched. I slapped my hand over my mouth as I stared at an old, decrepit wheelchair by the table. I gasped in shock. It was the same broken chair I'd crashed into in the wet, rotting hall of the Excited Ward.

"Where the hell did that come from?" My voice shook through my hand, which covered my mouth. Tears streamed from my eyes in terror.

Mom jumped off the couch, gazing wildly into the dining room.

"What are you talking about?" She whirled on me with piercing eyes.

I leaned to look around her, ready to ream her for not seeing it, but all that was there was the wooden armchair at the head of the dining room table.

I blinked in disbelief. My mind was playing tricks on me again. It must be exhaustion. And it was probably time for me to admit that my brain injury was rearing its ugly head again. This time, instead of intense rewiring, it was now hallucinations. I'd take the savant symptoms over hallucinations any day.

"Sorry." I brushed away my tears before she saw them. "The light hit the table funny, and I was sure I saw that old photo album I hate. I thought you were going to torture me with those evil portraits again."

Mom smirked for a moment, thinking of how much I hated my bucked teeth and bangs from second grade.

"You're rather jumpy," she said.

"Yeah, I know. I just need to lie down."

"Well, I don't want you going out anymore. For a few days at least. You need to follow doctor's orders, and I'm the one to enforce them." She stood over me now, casting her shadow like a blockade.

"Yeah. We'll see," I mumbled.

"We *will* see, Grace Frances. You'll do as I say."

"Mom. Just stop." My fists squeezed tight. "I'll rest now and see how I feel in the morning."

"You'll do as you're told, young lady," she demanded.

Rage built up in me, causing my face to heat up. It must have been blazing red. As I lifted my eyes to hers, red lines filled my vision. At first, I assumed I was seeing the color from my anger, but then my focus landed on the wall behind her. Large red letters scrawled along the wallpaper in spray-painted words that said, "HELP US!"

I shot up to my feet.

They were the same words I'd seen in the Excited Ward.

My heart rate beat out of my chest as my gaze moved farther down the wall to the final word.

In bright red, it shouted, "RUN!"

CHAPTER 13

My mother stared at me like I was the enemy. Her judging eyes scoured every inch of me as if she were searching for evidence of who I truly was. And based off the grimace that twisted her face, she didn't like what she saw.

"What's wrong with you?" she snarled.

I lifted a shaking finger to point to the wall behind her. "Don't you see it?" My voice trembled as I stepped away. "Can't you see?" I got louder.

She turned for a second, then whirled on me again. "See what? What the hell are you talking about? You're talking gibberish. Just like your father!" And her hand flew to her mouth in an attempt to catch the words before they hit the air.

My vision zoomed in, directly on her face. Her words had knocked the air out of me. Disbelief filled me at her callous reference to my father. She knew that was a vulnerable place to go, and she'd used it against me.

Swallowing, I glanced at the wall again. The red letters were gone, and I could only imagine she was right about me. Gibberish, she called it.

But I knew what it actually was.

It was the ward.

It had followed me home.

It had taken hold of a part of me deep within the hidden shutters of my mind.

"What do you mean?" My eyes narrowed, and I scowled. "How am I just like my father? Tell me."

She stumbled to the couch, then plopped down as if exhausted by the battle that was only just beginning. Her head shook as she exhaled for miles.

"He saw things, too," she murmured.

"W-what?" I stuttered. "What the hell are you talking about?"

"Don't you swear at me," she shot back.

"What are you saying?" I pressed.

"He saw things. Said things," she started. "He sounded crazy. Making predictions and having grandiose ideas."

Bewildered, I froze. I'd never heard so much about my father in my entire lifetime. And now, in two seconds, I was hearing that he was a babbling crazy person.

"Predictions of what? What happened to him? Where is he?" I begged.

She dropped her eyes to her lap, wringing her hands.

"Crazy talk. From the moment you were born," she said. "Made everyone uncomfortable. He'd lost his mind, Grace."

I pulled back from her in shock. How could she speak with such disrespect about him? Without any emotion or feelings?

"What happened to him?" I repeated.

She hesitated, but then said, "We needed to protect you from him. He had to be kept away from you."

"Where is he?" I pressed.

Her voice dropped to a whisper. "They sent him to the Blackwood State Hospital." She paused. "And he never came back."

A high-pitched ringing in my ears made me temporarily deaf. All of my senses morphed into a blur of cotton fog.

The Blackwood State Hospital? The asylum?

My father had spent time there. It couldn't be. How could he have been so close when I thought he was so far away?

I fell back into my chair, wishing for it to absorb me into oblivion.

If my father had spent time at the asylum, maybe that was why it was familiar to me. All the strange feelings that overwhelmed me on the grounds... maybe I'd been there before.

"Did I ever visit him there?" I asked in a small voice.

Her head shot up in confusion. "What? No. I would never let you see him in that wretched place. He was dead to us when he went away."

Her heartless reply shot rage through me. She'd cut him out of my life with no regard for his wishes or even mine.

My hands flew to my hair, and I pulled on it. "We abandoned him?" I screamed.

"No. He abandoned us," she shouted back. "He lost his mind and left us alone to survive on our own."

I couldn't believe the twisted words I was hearing. She had put her typical spin on the situation to make us out to be the victims. My stomach churned as sour sickness returned. If only I could purge this truth out of me. There was no way I could live with it in my soul.

"So where is he now?" I begged, desperate for more information.

"He died there, Grace." She paused. "A long time ago."

"No," I cried.

No. Closing my eyes, I fought the pain of sorrow that gouged at my chest. I never even had the chance to help him. To save him. Or to even know him.

Though, somehow, I'd never felt closer to him than in that moment. It was the first time I'd ever actually felt his true essence. His love for me.

I'd walked on the same grounds as my father. At the place where he drew his last breath. Alone.

My head felt like it was splitting down the middle.

"I can't handle this," I cried. "I don't know what to do with it." I paced the floor, still tugging at my hair. "Why did you never tell me before?"

"I was afraid," she whimpered. "Afraid you would be like him." Her voice cracked. "If you didn't know, then maybe you would be okay, I thought. But now, now you're scaring me with your strange behavior."

"Oh my God. Strange behavior? What the hell do you expect?" White-hot anger blasted through me. "I've been in an accident. I have a head injury. And now you tell me this? Of course it will be strange."

"No. Seeing things that aren't there…" she said. "*That's* strange. And that's what happened to him, too."

My eyes widened. He saw things, too? A sixth sense maybe, like mine. It was new to me since my accident, but maybe it was something he'd passed down to me.

My mother was afraid of such things, but I wasn't. I was more awake than ever with a sharp clarity that saw through her distorted web.

"What did he see? Mom, tell me."

She continued to wring her hands in her lap as she considered her words.

"He said he had to protect you. That you would be taken from him." She wiped at her nose. "He said he could see you suffering, trying to break out of a prison of some kind."

My spine straightened as she continued.

"His obsession about you being taken, being sent away, grew wilder every day. He wouldn't let people near you or even look at you. We had to have him sectioned before he had a chance to actually harm you." She sniffled. "You were still only an infant. Foster was mentally ill."

My mind exploded with the new knowledge of my father, including hearing his name. His intense protection surrounded me and lived on deep within my soul. He had wanted to protect me with all of his being, he'd done whatever was in his power to do so. But he'd lost. And he'd died believing he had let me down. The thought of it killed me inside.

"Foster." I spoke his name just to hear it again. "Do you think he was mentally ill? Or was he just desperate to protect me from something that frightened him? Something only he knew?"

The question was real. Mental illness was grossly misunderstood, even twenty years ago.

"Well, what in God's name could he have been talking about? It was all gibberish," she said.

In God's name? Had she had the church involved with sectioning him? How else could she have accomplished having him locked up in a mental hospital? My jaw tightened enough to crush granite.

"How did he die?" I asked through my clenched teeth.

She didn't answer, nor did she look up.

"How did he die?" I repeated, louder this time.

"He hung himself."

∼

Heavy sadness weighed down on me, drooping my shoulders and filling my neck. It was the exact same feeling I got at the asylum, more than once. I reached for my throat, rubbing it self-consciously.

My father had hung himself.

I strained to swallow, but the pressure in my neck made it impossible. My throat was too tight.

And Emma Grangley... She had hung herself too.

Tension built in my head as I struggled to take a full breath. It felt like I was being strangled by a noose.

I had to get out of there. I had to get away from my mother's twisted reality.

Pushing myself off the armchair, I stumbled toward my room, half-keeled over. Shallow breaths left me panting and searching for fresh air.

"Where are you going?" Mom asked, following me down the hall to my room.

"I'm getting out of here," I wheezed.

I grabbed my phone and jacket before pushing past her out of my bedroom door.

"You have to stay here," she demanded. "I'm calling your doctor." She scrolled through her phone with shaking hands.

It rang until the answering service picked up, then she ended the call. Within a second, she dialed Kaitlin's mom.

I shook my head in disgust, moving toward the front door. The rage inside me had built up enough energy to take me to Kaitlin's on foot. And I'd likely get there fast, too

"Cheryl." Mom's voice hit at the back of my head. "Grace is out of control. I need your help." Her panicked tone would easily frighten Kaitlin's mom, so I texted Kaitlin immediately to warn her as I flew out the front door. Mom's voice trailed behind me as if trying to get through to me. "She's behaving erratically and is delusional. I think she's on her way to your house. She'll upset Kaitlin, too, if you let her in. Cheryl! Are you listening?"

There was a good chance Kaitlin had already interrupted the phone call, pulling her mother's attention away from my mom. That was good. Hopefully, Cheryl would see through my mother's irrational angst and make her own decisions.

"Grace!" my mother called from where she stood on the porch.

I was already halfway down my street at a stride that carried me like the wind. My pounding heart set the pace, and I allowed the breeze to blow my hair back behind me.

"Grace!" Her voice grew more distant. "It's all gibberish!"

The words shot my eyes open. Had she actually said that? I couldn't be sure. It was difficult to hear her now, but I was fairly certain she'd said it. And it only sealed my conviction she was not the support I needed. She was the crazy one.

And right now, I needed rational.

I needed stable.

Before long, I pounded up Kaitlin's front steps. The door flew open. Kaitlin's mom reached for my shoulders, then pulled me into her. Her embrace choked me with emotion as I felt motherly compassion and understanding for the very first time. She trembled as she led me into the house, over to Kaitlin.

I stopped in my tracks when I saw Kaitlin. She sat on the floor by the fireplace, knees pulled to chest, and rocked. With a blank gaze, she hummed a quiet note as if trying to soothe herself.

My eyes jumped to her mom.

"She's been like this since she got home," her mother said. "I don't know what's wrong with her. Then your mother called, and I...I just didn't know what to say or what to think." Her eyes searched mine for an answer. "What did you girls do? Where did you go? Did something happen?" Her questions flew in every direction.

I hurried to Kaitlin, then dropped down next to her. With my arm wrapped around her shoulders, I squeezed her.

"It's okay, Kaitlin. I'm here," I whispered. "We need to stay together. I won't leave you until everything's normal again."

She blinked, lifting her gaze to mine. "Promise?"

"Yes." I exhaled with relief.

She was responsive. But she was scared, just like me.

I turned to her mother. Making a quick decision, I told her everything.

From the very beginning, I described our visits to the asylum and our strange encounters. I told her of Tom. About Emma. Every detail of our exploration of the shuttered ward and the ghostly grounds.

"It's what we love to do," I added. "You know how we like to explore old, abandoned houses and historical cemeteries? Only this time, it was bigger than we could have ever imagined."

Kaitlin's mom nodded, listening patiently.

I continued, "But our heads..." I rubbed the side of my face. "I think our head injuries are playing tricks on us. The symptoms, you know, the savant symptoms the doctor told us about, like our brains are opening up to new things. I think it's all related somehow."

Her mother pressed her knuckles onto her lips in thought.

Kaitlin lifted her head slightly. "It's true, Mom," she mumbled. "Grace is right. It's our minds playing tricks on us. It has to be."

Tears streamed down her mother's face as she came toward us. She wrapped her arms around the two of us, then buried her face next to Kaitlin's.

"I've been so worried," she murmured through sniffles. "The two of you have...changed. It has me so frightened, but the doctors keep telling me it's normal." She sat back and reached for Kaitlin. She pushed her hair away from her face, then tucked it behind her ear. Then she looked at me. "Kaitlin is better when you're around. You two need to rest. Maybe I could take you to that yoga retreat in the Berkshires for a few days? To get you away from it all."

Kaitlin shot up to full attention. "No," she pleaded. And her eyes locked onto mine.

I held her gaze, knowing we couldn't leave.

Knowing we had to go back.

~

Kaitlin's mother backed away as if she'd been struck. She hadn't expected such a forceful response from her daughter. Kaitlin had been practically mute since returning home from the asylum earlier in the day but now—now she was headstrong and adamant in her decisions.

I walked with Kaitlin to her room, twisting to see her mom. She just stood there, slumped shoulders, watching us walk away from her.

"It's okay, Mrs. Edwards," I said. "She just needs a break. We both do." I watched her swipe at the tears that threatened to roll down her cheeks.

She nodded, retreating toward the couch. Her limp body dropped into it. She lifted her phone close to her face, squinting to see the screen clearly.

Before long, I heard her hushed voice whispering about post-concussion syndrome and exhaustion.

"She's telling my dad," Kaitlin cringed. "Thank God he's out of town."

I wondered how her father would react to all of this. He'd probably think it was female troubles and brush it away. I supposed that wasn't so bad right now.

I texted my mom to tell her I was sleeping over Kaitlin's. There was no way I was going home at that point. I couldn't even imagine going home the next day, either. But for now, keeping her at a good distance was my goal.

"Are you okay?" I climbed onto Kaitlin's bed with her, then wrapped myself around her long, body-length pillow.

She propped herself onto her other furry pillows with a tired grin. "Yeah. I'm good," she said. "Minus the trauma of getting locked in an abandoned insane asylum. Oh, and freaky hallucinations following me around, even here."

"Hallucinations?"

"I don't know," she mumbled. "I think I keep seeing things from the ward. Like stupid things. The peeling paint on the walls. The musty smells. The creepy light coming through the windows. And just, the feelings, you know."

"Exactly," I agreed. "I'm having weird flashbacks, too. Like, more than flashbacks. It's so real."

We must have been more traumatized from being trapped in the ward than I had realized. It was terrifying on so many levels. The feeling of not being able to get out was even worse than the haunting vision of Emma and the scary halls. It was a feeling of being defenseless, like a tortured prisoner.

"Well, we can't both be going crazy," she said. "So, it's obviously something to do with our accident. My mom's right. My mom's right. It must be exhaustion."

"Definitely." I paused. "I guess."

Her eyebrows lifted. "You have another explanation?"

"My mom told me some pretty serious shit about my dad. I don't know if it's connected in any way. But it's weird. The timing."

I drew in a deep breath, then told Kaitlin about what happened to my father. She barely took a breath through the entire story. By the end, she was floored.

"Grace. I'm so sorry," she choked through her disbelief. "I can't believe it. How could she not have told you sooner?" She pulled her pillow closer, as if trying to wrap her mind around the story. "No wonder it felt so strange there. It's all connected somehow."

"That's exactly what I was thinking," I agreed. "And I need to figure out how. Or what."

"It all started with the accident," Kaitlin mumbled. She pinched her eyebrows together with her fingers as she thought. "We need to remember more." She strained. "Like the numbers. Remember the numbers that kept flashing?"

"Yes," I burst out. "235236235236." I watched the numbers move through my mind again like a digital ticker.

Kaitlin closed her eyes. "And there was more. A clock. I keep seeing it whenever there's a flash of light."

I closed my eyes to remember the flashbacks from the scene of the accident. As I searched my memory of all of it, the image of a clock jumped into my mind.

"I see it, too! I remember," I exclaimed. "An old clock like on a town hall or some important building. Its black hands were clear as day. It was…"

Kaitlin's voice joined mine in that exact moment.

"Four-thirty," we said in unison.

We jumped back from each other.

"What the fuck?" I whispered.

"Holy shit." Kaitlin rubbed her eyes, shoving her hands back through her hair.

I tucked my hands into my jacket pockets and squeezed myself, trying to keep from freaking out. My right hand pressed against a crinkled piece of paper, and I grabbed onto it. Pulling slowly, I removed the paper from my pocket. As soon as I saw what it was, I threw it on the bed between us.

It popped open from its hasty folds, and the words at the top shot out at us. "**MEDICAL HISTORY**". My spine stiffened as I bent my head for a better look. Blotched ink confirmed what I knew we were looking at. Filled onto the top line was her name. *Emma Grangley*.

I had shoved her medical record into my pocket when Braden burst into the locked ward to get us out. And now, here it was, right in front of us.

"Read the rest of it," Kaitlin said. "There was more."

I looked at her like she was nuts. I didn't even want to touch it, let alone read it.

I stared blankly at the paper, knowing I had no choice.

Propping it open, I spread it out on the blankets so we could both see it.

After the diagnosis and archaic 'prescriptives,' including hydrotherapy and orbital lobotomy, there was a large stamp at the bottom. It covered several lines of additional information with its capital letters that read 'DECEASED'.

Nausea washed through me as I strained to read the messy scrawl written beneath the stamp.

I spoke the words out loud, each one catching in my throat. "Deceased. Felon of herself. Cause of death, unvirtuous, asphyxiation, hanged by the neck." I grimaced at the callous phrases. "They judged her even in her death." My disgust oozed from every syllable, and I focused back on the sheet to read more. "Date, 9 July 1920. Time of death, 4:30."

My eyes shot up to Kaitlin's.

Four-thirty? The numbers exploded in my head.

The clock.

The old clock tower on the chapel. At the asylum. It was the same clock that flashed in our minds at the accident, though its image was much newer in the vision. It burst into my mind, beaming its face at me, calling out the time from the shuttered corners of my memories.

Four-thirty.

CHAPTER 14

I squeezed the long pillow, pushing myself into the corner of the bed against the wall. Emma Grangley's death notice sat in the middle of the blankets as Kaitlin and I averted our eyes. Flashes of the asylum clock tower continued to glare in my mind. Four-thirty. It was the time of her death. The clock tower tolled the harrowing moment, forever in our brains.

"It's like Emma wanted us to know she existed," Kaitlin mumbled.

"Stop. That's creepy." But I knew she right. Somehow, Emma *had* reached out to us. Her untimely death left her soul unsettled, wandering the asylum. Lost. "Do you think she haunts the place?'

"Yup." Kaitlin turned her head from Emma's medical document.

I thought about the visions of Emma we'd seen at the asylum. Her hanging. Walking into the doctor's office in the ward. Leading us to her medical information.

"I don't know. It seems more than that," I wondered. "Because it wasn't just at the asylum. It was at the accident that we first saw evidence of her. The clock tower." I glanced at Emma's medical paper for a brief second, to be sure it was still there. "It's like she made first contact with us in that moment. Both of us."

"You're freaking me out." Kaitlin's voice shook, and she jumped off the bed. "It has to be just a bizarre coincidence."

"Seriously?" I glanced at her through drooping eyes. This was more than a coincidence. "And what about the numbers? There has to be some significance to the numbers. They're connected to her in some way. Like she's trying to tell us something."

"No." Kaitlin stepped to the far corner of the room, shaking her head. "Stop. I can't. This is getting too weird. Like, it's moving out of control, like I'm losing my mind. Can we please talk about something else?" Her voice tightened.

"You know we have to go back, right?" My direct tone left no other option.

"Don't say that," she pleaded. "I can't handle that right now. Please."

"Fine," I agreed, knowing we needed a break from all of this. "But in the morning, we need to make a plan. Deal?"

"Whatever." Her eyes rolled as she stepped closer to the bed. "Put that away for now." She pointed to Emma's paper. "I can smell the musk of the ward off it."

A familiar chill jolted through me. I smelled it, too. The paper carried a powerful link to the ward. Not only the smell, but emotions too. Feelings of terror, abuse, entrapment, violation—they oozed from the paper, sickening my soul with their foul poison.

I folded the paper, touching it as little as possible, then pushed it into my pocket. Then, feeling its presence so close to my body, I whipped my jacket off and threw it into the corner of the room. Then Kaitlin covered it with a blanket. Then a pillow. She grabbed her square bottle of perfume, misting the area around the heap.

"I think we're good now." I chuckled weakly.

"If we go back, we need to return that thing," she whispered. "I don't want it anymore."

"Same," I agreed. "It belongs there, anyway. Sort of like a memorial to her memory."

"Okay, enough," Kaitlin interjected. "We're not talking anymore about this right now. I need a break." She threw one more pillow at the pile in the corner.

My phone buzzed, and I flipped it over to check. Braden's name lit up.

What r u up to tonight

"Braden wants to know what we're doing." I smirked at Kaitlin with a new sparkle in my eyes.

"My mother will never let us out tonight," Kaitlin exclaimed. "She's way too freaked out. Like, she thinks this is a medical emergency. And rest is the only thing that will fix it. I literally know we're trapped in here for the night."

I typed back.

At Kaitlin's

Ellipses rolled at the bottom right away as he typed back.

Wanna hang out I'm still with Nick

My eyes shot up to Kaitlin's. "They want to hang out."

"He's with Nick?" She jumped onto the bed and scrambled to look at my phone. "Shit! My mom won't let us out."

I typed back.

Being held prisoner at Ks. Cheryl won't let us out

Kaitlin bit her lip while staring at my phone for a reply.

What time does she go to bed

I smirked at Kaitlin as she fidgeted and bit her nails.

"Tell him ten o'clock," she said.

"But what about your dad?" I asked. "When will he get home?"

She smirked. "Two more days." She nudged at me. "Tell them ten."

A huge smile crossed my face. Kaitlin was hilarious. She acted all scared and nervous but still, somehow, she was always up for the next thing. Especially if it involved Nick.

I responded.

10

We waited, staring at my phone.

Ok we'll be there after that

∽

Kaitlin jumped off her bed. "Shit!" Her hands ran through her hair. "What if my mom catches us?" She paced the floor.

"It's okay, Kaitlin." I fanned my hands at her to calm her down. "We need to see your mom's expectations as guidelines." I smirked. "She wants the best for you. She's trying to be a good mom. But come on. We're in charge of our own lives."

She wrestled with what she wanted versus defying her mother. "I know. You're right." She bit her thumbnail. "I just don't want to hurt her."

"That's why we'll sneak." I grinned. "She'll never know."

Kaitlin pressed her lips together and glared at me. Then she moved to her window. "Help me with the screen. You know how this thing works."

I jumped off the bed as new adrenaline pumped through me. It wasn't the first time Kaitlin and I snuck out her window to roam the neighborhood, giddy on stolen freedom and exhilaration.

"I love you so much," I gushed as I wiggled the mountings of the screen.

"Shh!" Kaitlin stiffened. "Don't make a sound. My mom will know if she hears."

"I know. I got this." I loosened the fasteners all around the screen, then gently pulled it from the window frame. It was the actual window I worried about. It always stuck, and the crank made a ton of noise. "Let's wait to open the window later," I said as I placed the screen behind her desk. "After she goes to bed."

"I wish her bedroom wasn't so close to mine," Kaitlin whined. "She has ears like a hawk."

"Umm, hawks have good eyes," I teased. "I don't know about their ears."

"Whatever." She laughed. "Either way, my mom has got 'em."

"Remember the last time?" I giggled. "You went out first, but then I got stuck, trying to squeeze out after you."

Kaitlin coughed out her laugh. "Oh my God. I was sure we were gonna get caught. Your foot kept banging on the radiator."

"That was so much fun." I thought back to our crazy high school days. We had no idea how easy things were back then. Sure, the pressure of school and all the anxiety that went with it. But now—now the pressures were different.

"We're too old to have to sneak out the window. You know this, right?" Kaitlin's tone held teasing judgment.

"We are." I agreed. "But, literally, it's worth it. Just for the rush alone."

Fingernails tapped on the outside of her door and we jumped like skittish cats. The door pushed open and Kaitlin's mom poked her head in.

"You girls okay?" she asked. "Do you need anything?" Uncertainty filled her eyes.

"We're good Mom," Kaitlin said, and I sent an innocent smile to her.

She nodded. "Okay, well, you have a nice sleep. Everything will feel much better in the morning."

She closed the door and a moment later, the sound of her own bedroom door closing made us grin.

"She's probably gonna read for a while first," Kaitlin whispered.

"Let's make nachos. She'll never suspect a thing."

We crept to the kitchen like criminals, knowing we weren't doing anything wrong, but still feeling guilty. I turned the TV on, and we crashed on the couch in the family room. A huge plate of nachos and cans of Diet Coke balanced on the ottoman between us, and we inhaled the snack.

"Oh my God. I love this show," Kaitlin mumbled through a full mouth of chips and queso. "They're at a beach house and then their exes start arriving. The drama is so extra." She laughed at the bitchy girls in bikinis, stabbing each other in the back at every turn.

Between scrolling through Instagram and watching the show, we picked the nacho plate clean. Then my phone buzzed.

On our way

"Shit!" I grabbed Kaitlin's arm. "They're coming."

"It's barely ten-thirty." Kaitlin jumped up with a squeal. "What if my mom's not asleep yet?"

"We'll just have to be super quiet," I whispered. "Come on!" I grabbed the plate and cans, then got rid of them in the kitchen. We crept back toward her room as I typed.

Gonna sneak out her window. Park at side of house. Lmk when u get here

My heart pounded as we snuck to Kaitlin's room.

It wasn't like we'd be arrested or anything, but the thought of getting caught by her mother was still terrifying. She'd feel deceived and betrayed. All the stuff one would never want a mom to feel. It escalated the stakes even higher.

"Turn your music on and bang around a little while I try to get this open," I said as I lifted the lock on the window.

It rattled in its frame from the release of the lock, and my hands flew to my mouth. Kaitlin's eyes burst wide, and she jumped to her phone to start the music.

She moved her chair out from her vanity and dragged it around the room, making more noise than necessary. I went back to trying to open the window and gently pushed on the crank.

Every subtle movement of the lever sent a loud thump or vibration through the walls, and I cringed at every sound. Kaitlin paced as she watched every movement. I crouched with the next crank, squeezing my eyes shut, and bumped my hip into the wall with the following one to disguise the sounds. Each turn of the handle pushed the window farther open until it was wide enough for us to fit through.

I exhaled the breath I'd been holding the entire time, and Kaitlin blew hers out, too.

Cool evening air whirled in around us, and Kaitlin pulled on a hoodie. I moved to the pile in the corner, knowing my jacket was under the hoard, then raised an eyebrow at her.

She shook her head to stop me before reaching for another hoodie in her closet.

"No. Wear this," she said, blocking me from moving closer to the pile.

As I pulled the sweatshirt over my head, my phone vibrated.

We r here

It was the moment of truth. We had to escape from her window without waking her mother. It was near impossible as the window was a bit too high and the siding on the outside of the house made tons of noise, but we were determined.

Here we come, I typed back.

We looked at each other, and I nodded for Kaitlin to go first. She needed more help than me, so I boosted her onto the window ledge and held her steady as she leaned out of it.

The crank on the window caught on her yoga pants, pulling them down past her hip. Her red thong nearly glowed in the dim light, and a huge laugh threatened to burst out of me.

My hand flew to my mouth as I caught the laugh, forcing it to escape through my nose. The grumbling snort filled her entire room and we froze, with her hanging halfway out the window, in hysterical, silent laughter. I crossed my legs, nearly peeing myself as I struggled to release her pants from the crank. The more we laughed, the farther she fell out the window, making her pants come off even more.

There was only one solution.

I pulled her sneakers off and pushed her out. Her hands hit the ground and she walked herself across the grass on them, wiggling out of her pants. As her feet dropped to the ground, I threw her pants to her then covered my mouth, squeezing my nose to hold the laughter in. Tears streamed from my eyes while she struggled to get her pants back on before anyone might see. The fencing around her yard and the darkness were the only things that saved her from a full public exhibition.

Panting from the laughter, I stepped on her trash can and pushed myself up onto the sill. I looked back over my shoulder, to be sure her mom wasn't lurking in the doorway ready to grab me, then in a smooth motion, I pressed onto the windowsill and reached for Kaitlin to pull me out.

It was almost perfect. Until my feet ran along the outside of the house, rattling along the rows of siding. We froze, waiting for any sounds of her mother coming. I peeked through the window, but her door was still closed and the music kept playing.

"Do you think she heard?" Kaitlin asked.

I reached in for the crank to close the window as much as possible. "I don't think so," I replied. "We're good."

We snuck through the backyard to the farthest corner.

"The gate makes too much noise," Kaitlin said. "And its right next to my mom's window." We pressed in behind a bush. "This is safer."

After we climbed the fencing, we dropped over the other side. Our feet splatted on the cement sidewalk, and, following the smell of cotton candy vape, we ran for Braden's car.

CHAPTER 15

We opened the door to the backseat of Braden's car without making a sound and slid in. I pulled it closed behind us as quietly as possible until it latched shut.

Nick spun around, blowing a white cloud of sweet candy at us.

I waved the plume away from my face. "I could smell your vape from a mile away," I said with a fake cough, rolling my eyes.

Braden reached back to lift a bottle of blue raspberry vodka from the backpack between us. "Figured we'd need to celebrate the jailbreak."

Kaitlin glanced out of the car window in search of her suspicious mother. "Let's get out of here," she said.

"What, like drive?" Braden asked.

"Nah...we shouldn't go that far." She looked toward the house again. "Let's just walk."

She knew she'd be in less trouble if she was nearby, in case her mom noticed us missing. Plus, it was a beautiful night. And Braden had my favorite alcohol.

I never drank much, but when I did, blue raspberry Rubinov was my go-to. Something told me it was a bad idea with a head injury, though. But it seemed like a peace offering from Braden, in a way, to break the ice between us. So maybe I'd just have a little.

Braden put the bottle back in his backpack and we all crept out of the car, closing the doors behind us with gentle pressure from our bodies. Once we were a few houses beyond Kaitlin's, our volume rose and we moved more naturally. The idea of sneaking out made us all giddy, and we headed straight for our favorite spot—the turf field and playground at the end of Kaitlin's street.

Nick passed his vape as we crossed the street and moved into the open field. I shook my hand at him. I'd never gotten the whole vape thing. It burned my throat and made me jittery. Blowing out the white smoke was fun, but not worth coughing up blood.

Kaitlin, however, reached for it without the slightest hesitation.

Nick smiled as he passed it to her. It was like an invisible hook-up between them, judging from the time-lapse of his releasing it and her taking it. I nearly had to look away to give them privacy.

She lifted it to her mouth, then sucked on it. Nick watched without blinking. Then she blew the cloud out in front of her, swiping at it with her hand. She passed it back to Nick, and he immediately put it in his mouth for another hit. I averted my eyes this time.

Crossing the field toward the playground, Braden walked alongside me. "That was pretty intense today," he said. "Are you okay?"

Being locked in the shuttered ward seemed like a lifetime ago. It was hard to believe it was still the same day. "I actually don't know. It's like it hasn't hit me yet. Everything. You know... Like I need time for it to sink in."

"Makes sense," he said. "Maybe once you sleep on it, it'll calm things down a little." He paused, probably not knowing what else to say. "You're safe, though. So hopefully it won't, like, bother you."

He was probably wondering if I'd be traumatized from the event. He just didn't know how to say it. But somehow, I didn't think it would trouble me that way. I was more fascinated by the whole situation rather than traumatized by it. If I was scarred from it, I wouldn't have this primal urge to go back.

He pulled the bottle out of his backpack, then unscrewed the cap.

"Here, calm your nerves." He hesitated. "And to apologize for threatening to tell your mom." He lowered his eyes onto the grass. "I guess I panicked a little." He passed it to me for the first sip.

I smiled, thinking of all the times Braden and I found ourselves at parties with a little buzz. We'd always stick together and have the best time. Everyone always thought we'd hook up or that we had a secret affair, and it was obvious he would have in a second. Instead, though, we always just enjoyed our closeness. And our friendship. It was hard to explain or understand, but we'd always managed to avoid the hook up, no matter how close it came.

I thought it made our friendship more special. There was a deep trust that made me feel safe around him. His earlier reaction to me when we fought on my front lawn was just him trying to protect me. That was clear now.

I took the bottle from his hand. The blue raspberry taste masked the burning of the vodka as I took a sip and it moved down my throat.

I exhaled and passed it back to Braden. He took a sip, then handed it off to Nick.

I smiled as I watched him. Images of him bursting through the locked door of the ward, grave concern all over his face, replayed in my mind. His urgency in that moment was invigorating.

The vodka warmed me from within, sending a strange urge through me.

I wanted to wrap my arms around him and never let go. I just wanted to hold him. To have him hold me. It would feel so natural, with no effort needed. I started to ache for it.

The feeling was surprising. And overwhelming.

∽

Breaking away from Braden's hypnotic gaze, I ran for the wooden climbing structure.

A plank with scattered rock-climbing holds all over it led up to the hut at the top. I reached for the lumpy hand-holds, grabbed, then pulled myself up on the board. After I climbed all the way up, I wiggled into the child-sized cabin. Inside, benches jutted out from the walls surrounding a small round table in the center. I squeezed in along a bench at the far side, making room for the others.

Braden hopped onto the plank. In two effortless movements, he was at the top. He passed the backpack to me so he would fit through the small entryway.

Poking my head out the window, I called to Kaitlin.

"Get in here!" I laughed. "We have the Rubinov."

Nick pulled her away from the rock-climbing plank, and she giggled.

"Here I come," she called, resisting his tug.

Braden shuffled along the bench, trying to get a comfortable position. He hunched over, clearly too large for the play space. I chuckled at his clumsy fumbling, remembering the times we'd all come here years before, when we fit more easily.

"Remember when the police chased us from here?" he said. "We ran. We shouldn't have run." He shook his head at our stupidity.

"I know!" I chuckled. "It would have been no problem if we hadn't run."

"We hid in the bushes thinking we were all set," he added.

I remembered it well. We'd huddled together in the bushes, his arm around me to keep us as small as possible. We giggled quietly until the bright flashlight exposed us. Somehow, one of the cops had found us. Parents were called. Punishments were delivered.

"Those times were so much fun," I murmured. "We had no real concerns."

"Yeah." He nodded his head. "Good times."

I wondered what was keeping Kaitlin and poked out the window again. My eyes followed the white mist that trailed behind them. She and Nick were walking toward the darkness of the trees at the back of the field.

Oh my God. She was leaving me to go hook up with Nick.

My stomach flipped. She had always wanted to. I could never understand why—okay, his eyes—but other than that...

And now I was alone with Braden.

I was going to KILL her!

He reached into his backpack to retrieve the bottle. He passed it to me, wobbling it as if tempting me to take it.

My head was already spinning from my strange feelings and from being alone with him. "No, I'm good right now. You have it."

He put it back in the bag. "Nah, I'm good, too."

My stomach clamped as I saw him in a new light. I observed his features. He was handsome. It was no surprise all the girls wanted him. I'd just never allowed myself to look at him like that before. I guessed I'd never wanted to risk what we had.

Then, in the next breath, the clamp on my stomach loosened and my shoulders relaxed.

"Thanks for today," I said.

"Hmm?" He looked into my eyes.

"You know. For getting us out of there." I sent a gentle smile to him.

"Oh. Yeah. You're welcome." He fidgeted in his tight space.

Then a surge of bravery moved through me. I couldn't tell if it was the sip of vodka or something else, but it felt amazing. It was like the purest form of me had awakened, allowing the simplicity of truth to be revealed.

And the truth was—I had feelings for Braden.

I'd suppressed them for such a long time I'd lost touch with them. But right now, in this moment, they rushed to the surface and refused to be ignored any longer.

I bit my bottom lip in fear of what I might do. The feeling was so intense, like I was on a thrill ride that sent my head spinning.

"It's weird we've never…you know," I began.

His eyes widened to full attention.

I continued. "Why do you think that is?"

He shifted to turn toward me better. "I don't know," he started. "You always push me away, I guess."

I closed my eyes to avoid seeing his face. "I do? I don't mean to…"

"It's okay," he said. "I'm fine. I think it was probably a good thing anyway. It allowed us to stay close friends, you know, like we never had to be awkward or uncomfortable around each other."

"That's true." I looked at him again, grateful he appreciated our friendship as much as I did.

My eyes dropped slightly and landed on his mouth. A thrill shot through me as I imagined touching it with mine. And what it would feel like to kiss him. I tore my gaze away again in an instant before he caught me.

Too late.

He took a short inhale, pulling his bottom lip in. It glistened as he released it. His eyes held mine in a strong hold.

"Braden," I whispered in a final attempt of resistance.

And at the sound of his name, he reached up and touched the side of my face. He pushed his fingers through my hair and pulled me closer, leaning in to me.

"Grace." My name moved from his mouth and drew me into him.

His breath warmed my lips as he hovered just out of reach, as if waiting for a final invitation.

I couldn't hold back another second. As I reached my hand around his neck, he pulled me closer and his warm lips touched mine.

At first, he was gentle and reserved. He kissed me softly as if trying not to scare me off. But I wanted more. I wanted him to give himself to me fully, so I pulled tighter on his neck.

His entire body responded to my request. He inched closer and kissed me the way he had always intended to. With passion, without holding back. And I loved it. My mind swam in bliss from the thrill of his mouth.

"Grace!" Kaitlin's voice shattered my mind into pieces. "Throw down the bottle," she called up to us.

Braden pulled away, panting. Our gazes locked. "Oh my God."

Smiling, I fumbled through his backpack without breaking eye contact.

I leaned and dangled the bottle out of the window. Kaitlin reached up for it. It was obvious she could tell by the look on my face. Immediately.

Her eyes widened as her jaw dropped open.

My grin confirmed her knowledge, as she grabbed the bottle and ran over to Nick. The two of them headed back toward the trees, glancing over their shoulders at the hut in total disbelief.

I turned back to Braden with a smile on my face.

"Jerks," I said.

"Terrible timing." He smiled. And before I could say another word, he pulled me into his arms again. "Grace." My name poured from his lips as I became lost in his safe embrace.

∼

Kaitlin pinched my arm a million times in disbelief on the walk back to her house. I barely felt it, though. My mind was too wrapped up in Braden. I watched him walking ahead of us with Nick, and I regretted all the time I'd lost with him. But at least something was happening now. And it felt good.

"Who wants DQ?" Nick called. "Ethan's closing tonight. He can get us whatever we want."

"Yes," we replied in unison.

Kaitlin grabbed onto my arm. "I can't leave, though. If I get caught, my mom will be pissed."

True. Walking the neighborhood was one thing. But driving away was quite another. And we didn't want to piss Cheryl off. She was the only adult who had our backs at this point.

I called out, "We can't leave, though. Cheryl will kill us."

Braden slowed the pace with Nick, and we caught up to them.

"We'll bring it back then," he said. "What do you want?"

I smiled knowing he was buying more time with me.

"Oreo Blizzard, of course," I replied.

"Make that two," Kaitlin added.

They picked up their pace, moving well ahead of us, and were pulling away in Braden's car just as we reached the house. We fumbled at the gate, trying to open it without making too much noise.

Climbing over the fence from the outside was near impossible since the crossbeams were only on the inside.

Wood creaked as the gate resisted our efforts. Inch by inch, we finally pressed it open but only to cringe at the high-pitched squeak of the hinges. We crouched to stifle our nervous laughter before squeezing ourselves through the narrow opening.

"How are we gonna get Braden and Nick through?" Kaitlin whispered.

"We'll open it a little more in a few minutes," I said. "Just in case Cheryl's getting suspicious."

We snuck to the far side of the back yard where the lawn swing was and pulled some chairs close to it.

"Can we light the fire pit?" I asked.

Kaitlin hesitated. "I don't know. It might generate too much attention. Maybe we should just light some of the mosquito lanterns."

She went into the shed and pulled out a box of long matches and small tealight candles. We fumbled with the plastic lanterns, putting new candles in them, then lighting them. Placing them around the sitting area cast a warm glow, and Kaitlin shot a judging glance at me.

"Too obvious?" she said.

"What?"

"Romantic candlelight." She laughed.

"Shut up!" I punched her arm and then pushed her.

She pushed back and teased me with her taunting.

"I can't believe it," she said. "You and Braden." Her eyes went wide. "Finally!"

"Well, what about you and Nick? What the hell happened with you guys?"

The sound of Braden's car pulled up alongside the fence, and their hushed voices mixed with the shutting doors. Our shoulders flinched as if to buffer the noise, and we ran for the gate. Pulling the door a little farther open, we waved for the boys to follow us quietly.

Braden held the tray with the four blizzards, and Nick carried the backpack over his shoulder.

"Just don't wake my mom," Kaitlin hushed. "She's already freaked out today."

"Yeah, I can't believe you guys actually went back to the asylum," Nick interjected. "What were you thinking?" His judgmental tone irked me.

"We're going back again. Like, soon," I said in defense, staring into the flame of one of the candles.

"Wait," Braden interjected. "You're going back? Why?"

His annoyed tone hit me in the gut. It held a level of concern that scared me. But there was no way I wouldn't go back there. It had already planted itself deep within my mind, and I could think of nothing else. The only way to stop it's incessant stalking was to go back and face it.

"There's something about that place, Braden," I said. "Like there's something that needs to be found. Or discovered. I don't know." My words confused even me.

His eyebrows pulled together. "I mean, it's cool. Yeah. But I don't get why you need to go back so soon."

I poked a twig into the flame of a candle. "There's just so much mystery around it."

"Yeah, like the kid who killed his parents," Nick blurted out.

Braden dropped the tray of Blizzards onto the table with a huff.

My focus turned to Nick and I hung on his words, hoping for more information.

"I read about that boy, too," I said. "What else do you know about him?" Then I turned back to Braden. "What's he talking about?"

Braden handed me my Blizzard. "It's just some story Tom told us at the asylum. When we were trying to find you in the locked ward."

"The kid was found at the cliffs of the quarry," Nick said. "He jumped but survived. When they went to get his parents, they found his dad with a hammer in the back of his skull and his mother stabbed to death in the kitchen."

"Jesus," Kaitlin whispered.

We knew about the boy from our research but the article I had read didn't share such gruesome details.

"They kept him in the ward at the back," he continued. "The one with the high fencing. For the criminally insane."

I remembered the building at the far side of the grounds. Ward B.

"The weird part was," Braden added, "that the kid had no memory of the event. He had no idea what had happened. So, question was, did he truly have no memory of it or was he lying?"

"The kid did it," Nick blurted. "He was just a genius, keeping everyone uncertain."

"Maybe he *was* innocent," Braden added. "You gotta wonder how many people were trapped in there, wrongfully. Probably a lot."

Kaitlin scratched her arms like she had a rash and squeezed her eyes shut.

My eyes squinted in concentration, then closed as well, as I imagined the details of the story.

Then, a bright flash went off in my head. The boy's face.

It still had blood smears on it, with his dirty hair strewn in every direction, but his eyes remained calm. Focused. He appeared content.

My eyes burst open as I gasped from the shock of the image.

They connected with Kaitlin's as she stared into my face with similar fear. She'd seen the same image.

Then she whispered to me. "Do we know him?"

CHAPTER 16

There was no way we could know that boy from Ward B. The event was from decades earlier, long before we were even born. But Kaitlin saw it too. His face had flashed through our minds at the same time. Our reactions matched each other perfectly, and we knew what we'd seen. It was like we were being haunted. Haunted by the history of the asylum.

But it was more than that. And the need to know controlled my every thought.

"We're going back tomorrow," I said out loud, setting the plan in stone.

Kaitlin choked on her ice cream, but then she nodded in agreement.

Braden shoved his spoon into his cup and slammed it onto the table. "Shit." His lips pressed into a thin line. "I've never met two more stubborn people." His shifted his weight from one foot to another, then grabbed his ice cream again. "If you're going back, then I'm going, too." He huffed. "Not a chance I'm gonna just wait around for another distress call. That place has a weird effect on you guys."

"You've all lost your minds," Nick interjected, blowing a ring of vapor into the middle of us all. "But what the hell. I'll go too."

Braden opened his wallet and pulled a business card out of the billfold. "I'll text Tom. Let him know we're coming. Maybe he can be helpful. You know, be our guide."

I cringed at the thought of them coming with us. Braden was being over-protective and all he would try to do was stop me from getting into the ward again, or whatever else I decided to do.

"Thanks, guys, but you don't have to do that," I argued. "We'll be more careful this time."

But the more I thought about it, the more I realized so much of it was out of our control. Getting locked in the ward was a random coincidence, but being drawn in there by Emma, that was not.

I licked my spoon in thought. Maybe it was safer to have the guys come with us, even if it meant they'd be pains in the asses. Then, as I glanced over at Kaitlin to see what she thought, the worry lines in her forehead screamed that she wanted them to come.

"No, seriously," Braden started. "You can't go there alone. Look what almost happened when…"

I cut him off. "It's okay. You can come," I said. As the words left my mouth, my gut released its tight knot. "Thanks."

But now I had a new layer of worry. I had to worry about their safety too. They could be walking into something that could grab hold of them as well. There was just no way to know.

Kaitlin and I were tapping into something much bigger than Braden and Nick's minds could handle. They had no idea what was growing in us.

It was something unnerving.

Something sinister.

∼

The time between Braden and Nick leaving and then waking up to the bright glare of morning sun felt like seconds rather than hours. Twelve hours to be exact. It was almost noon, and my mind was still a shattered mess. Sleep didn't work at calming my thoughts. Rest didn't cut it. I needed something stronger.

"You awake?" I whispered, reaching for my phone.

Kaitlin squirmed in resistance to my voice.

I checked my messages and opened Braden's Snap.

"Three o'clock, right?" it said across the top half of his face.

"Yup." I snapped back a pic of the ceiling, hiding my morning face.

"Shit," I mumbled as I rolled off the edge of the bed. "They'll be here at three."

I still had second thoughts about them coming at all. It just seemed like something Kaitlin and I should do on our own.

Kaitlin's eyes burst open.

"Shit!" she squealed and sat straight up.

She reached for the side of her head and swayed like she was dizzy. Clearly, half-a-days sleep didn't do the trick for her either.

"Don't worry. It's only twelve." I searched around the room, on the shelves and in the closet. "I think we should be more prepared this time, like bring supplies and tools. At least a good screwdriver. And flashlights. Mace. And…"

Kaitlin squinted as if to see me more clearly. "Are you serious?"

"Completely."

She groaned in resistance to my enthusiasm. "Can I at least have coffee first?"

I chuckled and then shrugged my shoulders. Maybe I was acting a little extreme, a little too Indiana Jones, but my focus was clear. I wanted to be prepared at the asylum this time. I refused to be trapped like a prisoner or haunted like a skittish animal. I planned to be ready for whatever came our way.

"Didn't Braden say he was gonna contact Tom?" Kaitlin added. "If Tom's there, we'll be able to get into places without having to break in. No screwdrivers required. And he'll keep us safe, I bet. He seems to know every inch of the place. It'll be better this time. I can tell."

She made a good point. Maybe having Braden involved didn't seem like such a bad idea after all. Contacting Tom had been a good call since having more than just two people seemed pretty rational.

"And maybe we won't get trapped in one the wards this time," I snarked. "That would be cool."

I thought about what else Tom might be helpful with. Maybe he would have more details about the boy from Ward B. I couldn't shake that story, and it only muddied the images and feelings that already confused the shit out of me. And maybe Tom might know something about Emma Grangley. A knot formed in my throat. Or maybe even my father.

The more I thought about it, the more I realized we needed Tom. I silently praised Braden's forward thinking and his protective nature.

"Do you think Tom might know anything about..." I stumbled on my words. "You know, like, Emma. Or maybe my dad?"

Kaitlin pulled a pillow into her chest. "Holy crap," she gasped. "Maybe."

I glanced at my phone again. Braden hadn't opened my snap yet, so I double snapped him.

"Did you get in touch with Tom?" I typed over a pic of Kaitlin's feet.

I grabbed her brush and yanked it through my hair. "Nope. Not happening." I tugged harder. "I need to take a shower."

Kaitlin dragged herself off her huge bed, then hobbled into the hall. She came back with a fresh towel and said, "You go upstairs. I'll use the one in my parents' room. Cheryl's at work already and my dad won't be back until tomorrow." She dug in her closet and pulled out fresh clothes for me to choose from.

Heading into the bathroom, I looked forward to washing the past twenty-four hours off me. Kind of like preparation for the next events that awaited us.

After adjusting the temperature to the hottest setting just below scalding, I climbed in and let the water rinse over my hair and face. My eyes closed as my head tipped back, enjoying the escape of its trickling warmth. And then, with a flash, I jolted and closed my eyes tightly. Bright light blinded me at first but then the edges of an image formed in my head. It looked like a black and white shot at a first, like a transparent x-ray, but then a distinct face jumped closer and I yelped. Her face pushed right up to mine and I cowered as Emma stared straight into my soul.

My eyes shot open, and water streamed into them. I squinted and rubbed to clear my vision, looking all around me, ignoring the sting. Her face was still vivid in my mind, and she called to me. My heart pounded in my chest as I held the walls of the shower and gasped for air.

A vibration yanked my attention to my phone. It lit up on the sink, just within reach.

I grabbed the edge of my towel to dry my hand, then pressed the button to light up the screen. Braden snapped. I opened it and droplets fell from my arm and fingers, blurring the visibility.

"Shit," I mumbled, swiping the water off with my towel.

I read his snap through the streaks.

"K. Tom will meet us there." His words glowed against the background of his feet.

Okay. Everything was still normal. Braden was coming, and Tom would be there. I blinked again to remove the remains of Emma's face from my eyes. Her image had been so vivid, like she was in the room with me. My pounding heart proved her close proximity remained.

Goosebumps lifted on my arms. I pulled back into the hot shower and wet my hair again, this time keeping my eyes wide open.

My thoughts raced around what might happen at the asylum this time. It seemed good Tom would be there, but the knot in my stomach hinted otherwise. We had no idea who he was. He just seemed trustworthy and knowledgeable, but we had no proof. But seriously, who would hang out at an abandoned asylum that much? He had to have an element of weird in him. No doubt about that. Or maybe he was just as he said, intrigued like the rest of us.

I shampooed in a hurry, ready to get moving with the next part of the day. As I rinsed the suds, another flash shattered my peace. Emma's voice screamed in my mind. The sound of her shrieks tore at my brain like she was being tortured. Terror rang from her voice and I covered my ears with my hands. The sound moved through unhindered and its intensity compounded within me. I crouched to escape the horror she whipped through me.

Burning soap streamed into my eyes, forcing them shut again. I rocked under the stream of water, praying for the assault to end.

Body shuddering, I fell against the edge of the shower door with a bang. Emma grabbed at me. Clawing at my arms—desperate to be saved. I pulled to get away from her grasp.

"Get away from me," I screamed, swiping at the air.

What the hell did she want from me? I didn't know how to help her.

"Kaitlin!" I struggled to clear the shampoo from my eyes. "Kaitlin!"

My eyes refused to open against the stinging shampoo, and more flashes of Emma's twisted face taunted me. Her desperation clung in my chest, begging for my help, and finally, I stopped struggling. Instead, I stared into her searching eyes. I allowed her into my soul, and she allowed me into hers.

Her story poured into me, forcing my eyes open against the burning sensation. Her frantic thoughts continued to race through mine. Someone was after her as if they wanted to harm her. They used their power against her, and she had no defense. She needed me.

Then, a loud pounding on the door made me nearly jump out of my skin. "Let me in," Kaitlin yelled, smashing with rapid bangs. "Open the door!"

I fumbled on the doorknob with my shaking, wet hand as she screamed for me.

"Grace," she shrieked. Her terror-stricken voice shot more dread through my quaking body. "It's Emma! Stop her," she shouted, clawing at the door. "She won't get out of my head!"

∼

Kaitlin fell into the bathroom as her weight pushed against the opening door. Her cold, wet hair flew in every direction, and she landed on the mat, panting. Her towel barely held on as her body shook with massive quakes.

I grabbed for my towel and stepped closer to her, ready to help, but then froze. The after-images of Emma were still burned into my retinas. She was still there. Still…here.

"Do you still feel her?" I whispered.

Kaitlin's hands covered her face. "Yes," she whimpered.

I reached for Kaitlin's shoulders, then pushed to get her to sit up. "Look at me," I said. "She's here with us for a reason. We can't be afraid of her."

My own words surprised me. Every nerve in my body feared the sight of her. I'd do anything to erase her from my mind. But that was impossible now. She was in there, fully, and needed our help.

Kaitlin refused to open her eyes. "It's so real. It's like she's here," she whimpered.

"I know." I pulled her up more. "Come on. Let's keep getting ready. Let's show her that we are coming back for her. We need to stop resisting and let her lead us. It makes sense."

I had no idea why I wanted to let Emma in. It could be the same as leaving the portal of a Ouija board open and allowing the demons in. Disastrous. And the idea of her in our heads was terrifying. But somehow, it didn't feel like she was there to harm us. It was more like she was reaching out to us for help. And deep within me, I wanted to help her. I had to. It was the only thing that mattered now.

Kaitlin opened her eyes. "What happened to your arms?"

"What do you mean?" I looked down and gasped. Red streaks covered both arms, like scratches. "Shit. She was reaching for me. Grabbing at me."

Kaitlin's head shook like she didn't want to hear any more. "What's happening to us?" She wiped at her eyes. "Are we going crazy?"

"At exactly the same time?" I replied. "Doubt it."

It was possible I scratched myself when the shampoo was in my eyes, but really, I was convinced it was Emma.

"It's something else, Kaitlin," I added. "Something to do with our accident. Or the ward. Or both. I don't know. But I think we're about to find out."

My phone buzzed again.

Braden's text flashed on my screen.

on our way

I read it out loud. Had that much time passed already?

"They're going to think we're crazy," she mumbled.

"I know. It doesn't matter. They already do."

We scrambled down the stairs on our race toward her room to get ready.

Then, I added, "And that's why we're not going to tell them about this part."

CHAPTER 17

Kaitlin's mom had left a cute note on the kitchen counter next to bagels and strawberries. It told us to stay at the house and rest. It also asked for me to be sure to text my mom so she'd know what I was up to for the day.

We rolled our eyes at each other, grabbed coffee and bagels, and went to sit on the front stoop. Gray overcast shielded us from the sun and added a slight chill to the air, matching our moods to perfection.

I tore off a chunk of bagel and put it in my mouth. When I nearly choked on it, I placed the rest aside. My appetite had shut down completely.

"I can't eat," I grumbled to Kaitlin. "My mind's racing faster than ever. I can't stop it." I squeezed my eyes shut and pinched the bridge of my nose. "And the numbers. They keep flashing. And the hands on the clock tower just keep spinning. I need it to stop."

"It will. It has to." She took a large gulp of coffee and choked from the scald as it burned all the way down her throat. "Shit." She coughed. "We need to end it today. At the ward." She watched for Braden's car. "Whatever happens today, we need to face it. To end it."

I pulled back from her in surprise. I hadn't expected her to be so brave about the situation. About confronting it. We had no idea what we were walking into. But she was understood, we either had to end it now or be tormented forever.

But I couldn't help but feel like we were walking into something we knew nothing about. Something more powerful than anything we knew possible.

"There they are," she said as she hopped to her feet.

Braden pulled up, and Nick stuck his head out the window.

"Ready for ghost hunting?" he teased.

Little did he know he was as close to the truth as he could get.

"Ready!" Kaitlin called as we raced down the front walk.

Then I remembered my jacket. I ran back into the house to grab it from under the pile in Kaitlin's room. Replacing my hoodie with it felt like reconnecting with a missing part of me.

I hurried down the walkway, then jumped into the car. Pressing my hand into my pocket, I felt Emma's paper safe within. In relief, I flipped my head down and gathered my hair into a messy bun. I lifted it again, then tied my hairband around it. Braden's eyes were on me, and I smiled in response to his unexpected stare.

"You look good today," he said with a half smirk.

Nick turned to him with a scowl. "Aww thanks, sweetie."

Braden glared at him. "I mean, you guys look better. Like, rested."

"Yeah," Kaitlin interjected. "We slept for practically twelve hours. We better look rested." She glanced at me, knowing it was a load of crap. We'd never been more unrested in our lives, just teetering on the edge of our sanity.

I shook my head in a subtle motion as I thought about the irony. Here we were, barely holding on to our sanity after brain trauma, and on our way to visit an abandoned insane asylum. Were we nuts? It was like we were looking for trouble.

But we couldn't help ourselves.

The pull of the asylum was stronger than we were, and we couldn't resist it. We'd always had the curiosity to explore old, abandoned places. It was our passion. And finally it was clear that those adventures were only priming us for the big one. For this, now.

"Tom's gonna meet us there," Braden added. "He said he can show us another building and answer any questions. He was scheduled to be there for a maintenance shift anyway."

"I want to hear more about the dude who murdered his parents," Nick stated.

Kaitlin rolled her eyes, and I giggled.

My intrigue wasn't that far off from Nick's, though. The story of the boy from Ward B was fascinating. And I wanted to know more about Emma and maybe even my dad. The stories held within the walls of the wards were enormous, just dying to be heard.

Before long, I caught glimpse of the water tower that marked our destination. Braden knew the turns by heart, and I paid attention to the details of the surroundings this time. After passing the field with the ivy-covered black gate, the tires rumbled beneath us as we passed over old train tracks. They looked like they hadn't been used in years, but still cut their way through the town holding on to their own stories.

"I didn't notice tracks before," I mumbled.

Braden's head tipped. "There used to be a train station there. It's where they brought in the new patients for the asylum."

"Really?" I pictured the frightened faces of the new patients arriving.

"Yeah," he replied. "An image popped up when I googled the hospital. Showed them taking the patients up the road in horse-drawn carts. All the locals stood on either side of the road to witness the arrival of the new 'lunatics'. That was what *they* called them. It was like a circus."

"That's nuts." I heard a train whistle blow in the far distance and pressed my back into my seat.

The humiliation for those patients started before they even reached the grounds of the asylum. I was sure the spectators were awful. They probably taunted them and threw things as they passed through.

I'd seen a similar image from long ago on my phone, in my own brief research. But the dated, black-and-white photograph I saw was a line of women walking from the dining hall back to their wards.

Heads down. Hands folded. Long skirts. It twisted my stomach into knots, and I had closed the browser before seeing more. It felt odd now I hadn't gone back to do more research, but I supposed I hadn't had a moment's time yet. Seemed like Braden had, though.

"Did you find out anything else?" I asked while typing 'Blackwood State Hospital' into my phone.

"Yeah." He glanced at me in the rearview mirror. "A lot of stuff happened there that they didn't want the public to know about. Not just experimental therapies and shit, but like *psychotic* shit."

I kept my eye on him in the mirror. "Psychotic shit?"

He nodded and peeked at me again. "Yeah, like, *deeply* disturbing shit."

~

My head throbbed with a new pain I hadn't felt before. It could have been the screen-time while driving in a car, but I was more inclined to think it had to do with Braden's reference to deeply disturbing events of the past at the asylum. I knew there were stories to be found on the internet, but I didn't need those. Somehow, I already had them in my mind bouncing around, waiting to be deciphered.

"And we still need to find the cemetery," Kaitlin interjected. "If you think about it, it's what started this whole ordeal to begin with. We just wanted to find the damn cemetery."

I chuckled at the simplicity of our original plan. But now, it had grown into something much larger. A story that unfolded before us, telling each chapter as we went through it. And if these recent events have been the foreshadowing, then we were in for one hell of a climax.

Braden parked the car beyond the old granite sign for the asylum. My eyelids fell, thinking back to the new patients being carted up this same road, past that dreadful sign. It was their last moments of freedom, and they didn't even realize it. Until the gates closed with a clink behind them.

We climbed out of the car, trudging toward the entrance to the asylum. Shadows loomed over us from every direction, and a sick feeling of dread tightened my stomach.

"So what's the plan?" Nick asked. "We gonna try to find a forgotten prisoner? Someone still trapped in the high-security ward? Long beard, shredded clothes?" He laughed.

Braden turned to me, waiting for a response. It seemed he wasn't too sure what the plan was either and waited for my direction.

As we walked along the broken rubble of the old road, I realized there wasn't a plan. We just needed to return. That was all I knew for sure. And now that we were there, we would just have to see what happened.

"It feels weird we were so driven to return here again," I whispered to Kaitlin. "Like it pulled us back…taking our freedom with it."

My words sent chills up my spine. There was an intensity about the asylum. A sense of overbearing control that held us captive.

"Don't overthink it. You'll freak me out." Kaitlin wrapped her arms around herself.

As we reached the entryway to the grounds, Braden stopped and waited for me to reach him. His raised eyebrows asked for an answer to his previous question.

"Just tell me we'll be hanging out later, no worries, with all of this behind us," he said with a hopeful grin.

It didn't sound half bad actually. I wouldn't mind spending time with him later. No worries. All of this behind us.

"I need to get into the Excited Ward again." The words fell from my mouth before I even knew what they were.

"Fuck no," he yelled. "That place is dangerous. It's condemned for a reason." He shook his head at me. "Asbestos. Ever hear of that? Cancer?" He stared at me, waiting for a rational response.

"Well, I at least want to see what Tom can show us." I watered down my response to a level Braden would accept.

He hoisted his backpack higher on his shoulder, continuing through the remains of the original gates.

I hid the smile that threatened to spread across my face. He acted like he didn't want to be there or like he was the protective one, but it was clear he wanted to explore, too. His backpack had more than water bottles and protein bars. It probably had flashlights and tools, by the look of its bulk and weight. I smirked inwardly knowing he'd had the same thoughts about bringing pseudo-riot gear that I had back in Kaitlin's room.

"Do you seriously want to go back into the Excited Ward?" Kaitlin inched up beside me.

My head tipped. "You don't?"

It was a no-brainer to me. There was so much in there to be discovered. I was sure it held the answers we needed. The secrets it held screamed to make themselves known to us.

She shrugged, her gaze downcast. Her apprehension was normal, I supposed, but I didn't need her to flake now. There was too much at stake. Now was our opportunity to figure all of this out. Otherwise, we'd probably be tormented and stalked by these visions and the ward, for the rest of our lives.

"Hey, I think that's Tom's truck," Nick called from up ahead.

We moved into the grounds of the asylum, and the red brick buildings filled my sight. If not for all the boarded-up doors and windows, I would think we'd entered an ivy league college campus. The initial bucolic impression surprised me every time. Almost like a disguise for the treachery that truly lurked behind the shutters.

My eyes immediately shot to the clock tower that rose from the side of the chapel. The black hands that spun in my mind were missing, fallen off long ago, but vivid in my memory. Kaitlin, too, stared at the clock.

"He's there," Braden said, pointing to the loading dock of the dining hall.

He waved his arm to Tom, who was sitting on the concrete platform, waiting. Tom stood and walked toward us with a slow, relaxed stride. We moved along the road with the women's wards along the side and closed the space between us.

Just as we approached Tom, close enough to see his friendly expression, we all fell silent. Tom slowed just in front of the Excited

Ward, waiting for us to join him there. But something had shifted, changing our initial pace.

A heavy weight pressed down on me as we passed the first ward on the right—the one before the Excited Ward. Our nervous chatter shut down to full silence as we crossed in front of the ominous, dark building. Fighting the sensation of being rendered mute, I swallowed hard, trying to speak. It was like being caught in a nightmare where I couldn't scream. My voice was gone.

My heart rate accelerated as pressure constricted my neck. I glanced toward the tree where we'd seen Emma hanging. And I reached for my throat and rubbed it. I watched the others as we passed by the dark ward, and their shoulders slumped while their steps dragged. Kaitlin nearly fell forward to stagger past it.

As we moved closer to Tom, the cloudiness in my head cleared as I took a deep breath. The pressure in my neck released, and I coughed. The sound of my voice came out with a gasp.

"What the hell was that?" I blurted, rejoicing from the sound of my own voice. I looked behind me for any evidence of what could have had the power to steal our voices like that.

Tom stepped forward, nodding toward the building we'd just passed. "That one," he said. "It's the Quiet Ward."

◈

Kaitlin bent over coughing, and color returned to her blanched face. She glanced up and from the corner of her eye, shot fear into my soul. I nodded to let her know I'd felt the powerful effect of the Quiet Ward as well. It had silenced us all.

"I'm intrigued you wanted to come back here." Tom directed his comment to Kaitlin and me. "I'd have thought you'd have had enough, after what happened yesterday."

Before I could respond, Braden retorted.

"They never have enough. Always pushing it to the next level." Then he settled a firm stare on me.

My blood boiled at his cynical remark, and I fired back.

"We're not easily frightened off," I said to Tom, knowing full well the comment was a jab at Braden.

"Even when taking it to the next level," Kaitlin murmured in my ear, and I elbowed her in the ribs.

"Okay, well, thought you might want to see a bit of the chapel or maybe the research laboratory where they practiced new treatments on the patients." Tom pointed to the buildings across from the row of women's wards.

My eyes trailed back to the Excited Ward and scanned its boarded windows, searching for any new weakness I'd missed previously.

I turned back to the group, catching Tom staring at me. He gave a subtle shake to his head and lowered his eyes, as if to suggest we wouldn't be going back in there.

Now I was pissed we'd contacted him at all. If he weren't here, we could find a way into that ward and…

"What about the ward for the psychos?" Nick asked. "Can we get in that one?"

Tom pressed his lips together in response to Nick's disrespect and said, "That building's too far gone. It's not structurally sound. The committee's talking about razing it."

My spine straightened as my eyes shot to full alert. "What? They can't do that!"

The thought of them destroying any of these buildings terrified me. How could they even think about destroying something so…beautiful.

I glanced at Kaitlin and she held the same look of concern on her face.

"Why would they even think that was an option?" I continued. "This place needs to be preserved. It's full of history, and it's still so, so alive."

My words hung in the air between us all, trapped in the awkward gazes of everyone staring at me. I listened to them again and swallowed hard. I sounded like a lunatic to anyone who didn't understand. And quite possibly, Kaitlin was the only one who did.

Tom stepped closer. "I agree."

I stared into his face, trying to determine who he was. Did he love this place as much as I did? His volunteerism—he was committed to this place as much as I was. More, even.

"Why do you like it here so much?" I asked him.

He put his hands in his pockets. "I've always felt a connection to this place. Like it needs someone to care for it. Someone to protect it. Without me, it would have been sold long ago and turned into cookie-cutter condos."

The thought chilled me. "Well, thank you for looking out for it. It needs you."

"Yeah. It's kinda my side job at this point, in my retirement. Just can't walk away from it, I guess." He pulled his keys from his pocket. "So, what do you all want to know about the place? I've pretty much got the entire history up here." He tapped on the side of his forehead. "Worked here long enough to stow away a fair bit of intel."

I stepped closer to him, my stare dead-on.

"I want to know about Emma Grangley," I said.

Kaitlin moved closer by my side.

Tom's eyes darted to the hanging tree as if by instinct, then returned to mine with an uneasy look of dread.

CHAPTER 18

Tom's eyes shifted to the Excited Ward, then back to mine. His unsettling surprise at hearing Emma Grangley's name was written all over his face. He'd looked at the hanging tree and then at the ward. He knew something. Or everything.

"I don't know much of the actual patients, but I can tell you about the history of the..." His rambling didn't distract me from what he'd already exposed.

I moved up to him, shoulder to shoulder, and whispered, "You *do* know."

He pulled back slightly and examined me, as if calculating how much to tell.

"This way," he began again, then took a few steps toward the chapel. "The chapel was a place for service on Sundays but also for..."

I cut him off again. "We're not here for the formal tour, Tom. No offense. But I already know too much about this place. Way too much."

He gave a subtle nod, then continued. "You'll see that the benches had extreme straight backs and the seats were far from any level of comfort."

We approached the chapel and stepped onto the large stoop, overshadowed by a protective archway. Tom wiggled his key into the padlock on the oversized double door and snapped it open.

We all stepped back as Tom pulled the huge black doors, as if removing the seal of a centuries-old tomb. The stink of musk and mold wafted out first, and Tom waited a moment to allow the fresh air in.

"Please don't disturb anything, but feel free to have a look around," he said. "It's important to me to share these places with the public, to be sure the asylum's never forgotten."

We moved through the doorway of the chapel, and the sound of our footsteps echoed inside the cavernous space. It was like stepping into a time machine. Flying buttresses and row after row of hand-carved wooden pews. A simple altar stood at the front, cold and unforgiving. A chill ran through me as I imagined seeking repentance in a space so filled with judgment from the highest power.

The guys wandered toward the altar and stepped up to it.

"Tell me your sins, son," Nick boomed, standing as tall as he could.

Braden rolled his eyes and leaned in. "I had dirty thoughts, Father," he whispered. Clueless that his deep voice reverberated through the entire building.

"Blasphemy!" Nick taunted.

Idiots.

I moved up along Tom's side and spoke in the lowest tone possible. "Can you tell me about Emma Grangley? I need to hear whatever you know."

His eyes narrowed. "Are you a relative? What's your connection?"

"No, I don't know her, really." I stumbled on my words. "I found her name in the Excited Ward and well, I just want to know more about her."

He nodded and took a moment to think. "I am familiar with her."

I turned to see where the boys were. and saw them sitting on the stairs of the altar, waiting. Bored. Kaitlin had wandered over to them and reached for a sip of Braden's water.

"Can you tell me about her?" I asked. "Like, why she was here. What happened to her."

He thought for a moment. "I'm afraid she was one of the unfortunate, forgotten ones. Sectioned against her will, likely for offending her family reputation rather than true mental illness. That was the way back then."

I nodded, knowing it to be true. "What else? What happened to her?"

He hesitated but then caught my intensity. "She was kept in the Excited Ward as one of the 'disobedient ones.'" He rubbed his chin, considering his words. "Patients in the Excited Ward were restrained to the beds or sent to solitary for indefinite amounts of time. The sane became insane very quickly." He paused. "I believe she was one of the fighters. You know, strong-willed. They prescribed a lobotomy to subdue her."

I knew it. Her medical papers said the same.

"How could they do that?" I whispered.

"It was their way of keeping the patients under control in the overcrowded conditions," he added. "They'd end up in the Quiet Ward after the treatment."

Oh my God. My stomach turned.

"But she never got the lobotomy, right?" I said.

His chin pulled back in curiosity, but instead of asking me how I could know that, he went on. "That's right. She hung herself before they could carry out the procedure."

"At the tree by the ward," I stated.

His eyes narrowed, and he stepped away from me. He turned to the others and called, "Let's move out. Best not to disturb the calm in here for too long."

In a matter of moments, we were outside. Tom clamped the padlock onto the arched doorway, beads of sweat shimmering on his brow.

Kaitlin grabbed my elbow, pulling my attention to her. "What did he say?" she whispered.

"I'll tell you everything in a minute." I hushed her. "He knows about Emma. I'm not sure how much else he knows, but if you can keep the guys away a bit, I'll try to get more information."

"Got it." She moved closer to the guys. "You wanna see the research lab?" she enticed them.

I turned back to Tom hoping to get his full attention again. It was still hard to tell how much he knew, but my acquired sixth sense was definitely picking up on something extra.

"It's like I felt her here," I said, testing how far I could push him.

He regarded me with worry in his eyes, like I'd gone somewhere I shouldn't. And then warned, "I feel her here, too. All the time."

～

My hand flew to my mouth and covered it. Fear moved through me like ice as I realized Emma's presence was all around us. Even Tom felt it.

My curiosity exploded on how much he knew and if he felt the presence of other patients as well. Could he see them too? Would he be willing to admit it, even if he had? I was still sane enough to know when to filter my thoughts and experiences, but Tom was different. He could be a link to all of this.

"Have you ever seen her?" I asked, barely able to look at him.

He gazed back at the hanging tree. "No. I don't think so. Sometimes I'm not sure, but...the mind can play funny tricks in a place like this."

"Yeah. It sure can."

"Why, have you?" he asked.

"What?" I fidgeted.

"Seen her?"

"Oh, umm, no, well, I guess, I'm not sure, really." I stumbled on my words, uncertain how much to say. Tom listened with every part of his being, focusing on each word as if waiting for one in particular. A yes, maybe. But then my mind cleared, and my focus fell to my father. "Do you know of other patients, too?" I asked him.

I couldn't help but jump to my father. My brain just made the switch on its own, leaving me no choice but to follow its lead.

Tom was likely the same age as my father, or as he would have been. Maybe he would know something about the patients from not so long ago.

I pulled courage from deep within me and spoke of my father's time here. "I think my father was sent here when I was small."

Tom's eyes widened. "Really? When?"

"Well, about nineteen years ago. Basically, right after I was born." It was pretty easy to be precise with the timeline.

"That was during the time when I worked here." He stood taller with pride. "The men's wards were the last to remain open," he said. "Only two of them, housing patients who were well enough to care for themselves. More like halfway houses, you could say. They finally closed for good just around that time."

I took a deep inhale. "I believe his name was Foster."

I wished I had a last name for him now. I hadn't ever thought to ask my mother. I only knew she had dropped his last name and taken her maiden name for both us. But now, it was the only thing in the world that mattered, because in that moment, I realized it was my name too.

Tom halted his steps toward the research building. He looked back toward the hanging tree again. His gaze hovered on the tree, seemingly lost, as his hands began to shake.

My jaw dropped. He knew something.

"That was the year, just before the facility closed altogether. A man named Foster hung himself from that same tree." Tom's voice shook. "He'd cry out every night for God's mercy, asking for His grace. But even the grace of God couldn't have saved him that day."

I gasped in shock, and tears filled my eyes. With one blink, streams poured down my cheeks.

"Could it have been your father?" Tom asked. "It's an unusual name, one not heard often in those days."

I searched for my voice, trapped in the endless maze of my spiraling mind.

"It was," I choked out. "It was him."

Tom stiffened. "You're sure?"

"My father hung himself here. I knew that. But that's not how I'm sure." I hesitated and glanced back at the tree. "He wasn't calling out for God every night. He was calling for me. My name is Grace."

Tom wiped at his sweating brow, shifting his weight as if trying to absorb the magnitude of the situation.

"I'm sorry. I..." he started.

But I didn't need his sympathy. I just needed more answers.

"What happened to him?" I pressed. "How did he lose hope enough to want to die?"

Tom hesitated, staring at the others. They walked around the perimeter of the research building, looking up at its shuttered windows. Then he said, "He used to come to the tree every day. No one questioned it. It was as if he was drawn to it. But I knew different. It was like he had a sixth sense and felt something from it."

I thought of my own new sixth sense. And the visions of Emma that it brought to me.

"What do you mean, sixth sense?" I choked.

"It's going to sound crazy, but he would say Emma's name. Like he knew it was the tree she hung herself from. He would say she was in his head, trying to get to his daughter, and he would do anything to protect her, you, from her."

I stepped back in horror from his words.

My mother had told me he went crazy, trying to protect me. And now I had to believe it was his visions of Emma that frightened him. She had been in his head, too, but he had no understanding of it. She haunted him, trying to get to me, enough to make him appear like he'd lost his mind.

Emma had been trying to find me, even when I was a baby.

My knees wobbled beneath me, threatening to buckle completely.

"Is there a connection?" Tom asked. "Does any of it make sense?"

I shook my head, too scared to reveal what I knew. "I don't know. It's too much to take in," I murmured.

My spine stiffened as I studied the tree. The image of Emma's lifeless body hanging from the branch returned to me. It was blurry and faded at first, but as she slowly spun at the end of the rope, her face became clear.

As I focused on her purple, bloated features, a scream formed in my throat as her face morphed into that of a man's. The eyes were open and fogged by death, but the vivid blue color, speckled with golden hues, was clear as day. I recognized him as if I were looking into a mirror.

And then the scream reached my mouth.

Just before it blasted out of me, Tom's voice hit me right between the eyes.

"I remember now. His full name," he shot out. "Foster Frances."

∼

My guttural scream brought everyone running. They surrounded me and Kaitlin grabbed my arm, shaking it. Braden held my shoulders as his voice begged for an explanation. I dropped down to a squat, hiding my face in my hands.

Foster Frances. The name struck me with a force that nearly leveled me to the ground. My own mother's irritated voice scraped at my brain. "Grace Frances, clean your room. Grace Frances, do not disrespect me." She'd use my middle name only in times of anger or disappointment in my behavior. The name of her annoyance was Frances. And it was my father's last name. And now his face had been revealed to me as well.

Braden lowered down to my level, then whispered gently, "What is it, Grace? Something scared you?"

Leaving my face hidden in my folded arms on my knees, I collected myself as best as possible. There was no way I could explain what I just saw to Braden. I needed to convince him I was okay so I could get to Kaitlin.

I imagined Tom was probably freaked out as well, so damage control was my current priority.

"Sorry," I mumbled into my knees. "I'm embarrassed. I kind of spooked myself. Seriously thought I saw a ghost in one of the chapel windows. Dumb I know. I'm just creeped out right now. Big time."

"You scared the shit out of me," Braden said. "It sounded like a death screech."

"Oh my God. I'm sorry." My voice muffled through my sleeves. "I let my mind run away with me."

Tom stepped closer. "I think we all have, a little bit. But that's the fun in it, right?"

His words sounded like he was trying to help. Trying to redirect everyone's concern off me. But why?

My eyebrows pulled together as I homed in on Tom's mellow voice. He continued to distract the others with stories of neighbors hearing screams at night. Saying I wasn't the only one who had a vivid imagination.

I wiped at my tears. Pulled myself together. As he stood, Braden reached for my arm to keep me steady.

"I'm fine," I gently pulled away from his grasp. "I totally freaked myself out. I'm better now." I smiled, attempting to brush off any scrutiny and unwanted attention.

"So let's have a look at the lobotomy labs," Nick interjected.

Tom shook his head at Nick's crass tone, but he smiled and led us back toward the research building.

Kaitlin scrambled up to me. "What the hell happened? Did you see something?"

I hushed her with my hand. "Hang on. When the others are more distracted. You're not going to fucking believe this."

Her fist went to her mouth, and she bounced nervously as she considered whatever it could be.

Tom brought us up the crumbling cement stairs to the side door of the research building. It held the least architectural features of any building on the grounds and the only decor worth looking at was the crooked green lamp that protruded from the bricks, just above the stoop. I imagined its glaring light examining and judging the poor patients who were led into this building—headed toward their demise.

I wasn't even sure I wanted to go in, the feeling in my gut sent warning signals. The events that occurred in the past, malpractice and unethical treatments, all without patient consent, made me sick to my stomach. But it was clear this was the most fascinating of all the buildings to the guys at the moment. Braden and Nick nearly bounced out of their shoes as we waited for Tom to open the door.

As soon as the padlock was removed and the thick metal door pulled open, the three men stepped inside. Kaitlin and I waited a moment on the stoop, hesitant to go in.

"Come on," Braden called as Nick moved ahead without hesitation.

Kaitlin and I stepped inside, then allowed the heavy door to slam behind us. A hollow chill ran through me as the sound resonated around my body, like the sealing of a coffin. We shuffled along the tiled hallway to catch up to the others.

"What ever happened to the kid in the psycho ward?" Nick asked Tom. "Did he just rot away there?"

I cringed, embarrassed by my friend's disrespectful approach. But it made sense Nick and Braden would be obsessed with that story. It was the closest thing they could identify with since the boy was similar in age to them when he was sent there.

"Yeah, his was an interesting case," Tom agreed. "He seemed like such a normal kid. An athlete and a college student. They actually built a basketball court here on the grounds, just for him."

"Oh, I saw that court near the dining hall," Braden added. "The hoop's still there, broken and rusted."

"Right," Tom added. "That was it. He would shoot hoops all day. His treatment never seemed to make a difference for him. He continued to claim to have no memory of the murders."

"Do *you* believe he had no memory of it?" Braden asked. "Or do you think he was faking?"

"I guess we'll never know," Tom replied. "The effects of psychological trauma can cause the brain to react in different ways. Memories can lapse in the mind, causing someone to wonder if they were real or only a dream." He moved down the corridor while telling his story. "His therapist thought he'd made a breakthrough when the boy started speaking of a past life. He claimed he was abused and neglected in his prior lifetime and that in his new one, he had a clean slate." He shook his head. "The therapist believed he was perhaps trying to shift blame of his criminal actions onto someone else. Taking responsibility was too much for his mind to handle."

I listened to his story as best I could, while trying to make sense of what I had experienced outside by the hanging tree. It was too much information, and I desperately needed to process with Kaitlin. I slowed my pace so she and I could drop back slightly.

Tom's voice continued to bounce through the empty corridor, telling more of the boy from Ward B. Something about hidden tunnels beneath the wards and cavorting with the female patients. As the guys moved farther along the length of the hallway, their movement caused swirls of dust to waft through beams of light that broke through the open doors on either side.

"Did they ever let him out?" Braden asked.

"No one's entirely sure," Tom said. "Some say he killed himself for lost love. But most stories say he was used for psychological studies on brain function. They say he claimed his mind had been opened by the treatments, allowing experiences from the past to come through. Like events from before he was even born."

"His past life?" Nick blurted out.

"Actually, yes." Tom led them to the end of the corridor. "The clinical trials were to blame for his delusions. But the kid always claimed his soul carried prior life experiences, like he was reincarnated. His experimental treatments were never marked as illegal, but in hindsight, you have to wonder what they ultimately did to him. It was brain damage, really."

Braden and Nick soaked in every word and asked more questions, but I stopped in my tracks, hearing my own version of Tom's story.

My head injury wasn't so different from what that boy might have experienced. My doctors called it acquired savant syndrome—a rewiring of the brain that would allow for new abilities—my new sixth sense. Kaitlin's, too. It was like a window had been opened into the past, allowing information through, like flashbacks or deja vu. Just like that boy had said. But of course, he was a psychotic mess. Probably a murderer. I still couldn't help but see similarities in his thinking, though.

I stared through the crack in one of the doors along the side, lost in my own train of thought. I hadn't even registered what my eyes were seeing within the closed off room, when Nick's voice blasted through my skull.

"Holy shit! Is that where they did the lobotomies?" he called out.

∼

Nick's voice caused my eyes to focus in on what I was actually seeing. The door inside the research lab was cracked open just enough for the natural light to come through into hall, and I gazed into an examination room of horrors.

A silver-slab table was screwed to the floor in the middle of the room. Shredded straps hung from the sides. Rusted buckles stained the tiled floor, and old-fashioned machines sat on metal tables at the edges of the room. Round glass dials and gauges covered the antiquated meters, and red and black wires entangled the machines like cobwebs.

I stepped back and bumped into Kaitlin. She was leaning in for a better look as well when Tom's voice stole our attention.

"They would use pick-like probes in the orbital socket and scrape away at the brain," he explained. "This was all done well before ultrasound, so they had no guidance or accuracy at all. The patients would complain of headache afterward and were recommended to wear sunglasses as their remedy." He looked back down the hall at us. "They were moved to the Quiet Ward soon after."

I glanced back into the room, imagining what it would be like to be restrained to the cold metal table watching a probe coming straight at you. Terrifying. Violating.

I grabbed hold of Kaitlin and leaned on her. My mind swam with disturbing thoughts, and I recalled Braden's words from earlier. He said his research had disclosed 'deeply disturbing' information. His words barely touched the truth.

Tom hovered at the end of the echoing corridor while explaining hydrotherapy and a woman who died after being forgotten in the water. Some say she was boiled to death while others claim she died of hypothermia. Either way, I'd heard enough.

"Kaitlin, I can't stand being in here." I held her arm for support. "It has a horrible negative energy. Not like the ward. It has its own terrible feeling."

"I agree," she said. "This place is a house of horrors and we're walking straight through it." She gazed up the walls at the peeling paint and brown water stain streaks. "Let's get out of here."

I nodded, cutting my gaze to the end of the hall. The guys were gone. All of them.

"Braden," I called. "Nick. Tom?"

There was no answer.

"Shit. Braden!" I yelled louder. "Maybe they took the stairs."

We hurried to the end of the corridor and looked into the stairwell. It went down into pitch darkness and up into a narrow space of anti-suicide cages. Even in this place, patients would make a break for it. 'Acts of volition,' Tom had called them earlier. He said it was when a patient suddenly behaved in an unexpected manner, like throwing themselves down a stairwell, several stories high. Orderlies were instructed to always keep the patients in front of them—to never let them out of their sight.

Death was better than enduring violating treatments without consent, though. I didn't judge the choice, even for a second.

I hollered up the shaft. "Braden! Nick!" No answer.

"What the fuck?" Kaitlin said.

"I don't know," I murmured, listening with every ounce of my being. "I can't hear them. And there's no way I'm going up there. And definitely not down there."

"Same," Kaitlin agreed. "Let's just get out of here. I need the freedom of the outdoors right now. Like, right now."

Without hesitation, we turned and hurried along the corridor toward the door where we'd entered. Passing the room with the metal table, I kept my eyes forward, avoiding looking into its horrors again.

Turning back, with my hand on the door to our exit, I called one more time. "Braden!" And then burst out onto the cement stairs that crunched with loose gravel beneath my feet.

"Where the hell did they go?" Kaitlin panted, sucking in fresh air.

"They're just following their noses, lost in the intrigue of lobotomies," I said with a snide tone.

I was beyond pissed off. They should never have lost sight of us. I thought back to our first visit when Kaitlin and I snuck out of the dining hall, causing them to panic. Hadn't they learned their lesson then?

My eyes trailed up the brick exterior of the chapel in front of us and landed on the clock face. Its faded, peeling facade yearned for the days when it proudly displayed the time.

Then my attention turned behind us, toward the women's wards. I stared at the Excited Ward, narrowed my eyes to see more clearly.

A gasp escaped my lips as I grabbed onto Kaitlin. I stared at the front of the ward at a shadow that ran along the edge of the board at the entryway door.

It appeared to be slightly open.

CHAPTER 19

I squeezed Kaitlin's arm for a reality check as I stared at the front of the Excited Ward. An ominous shadow ran along the boarded-up entryway, making it look like it was open a small bit.

"Do you see that?" I pointed to the ward. "Is the door open?"

Kaitlin's body stiffened. "Maybe," she whispered, peering across the way.

I pulled on her as my feet carried me in a direct line toward the luring ward. My breath increased in speed as my pace accelerated. Nearly panting, my panic rose with every sharp inhale.

We crossed the crumbled road between the chapel and the women's wards, then stopped right in front of the Excited Ward. Staring at the entryway door, our shoulders slumped as heavy weight pushed down on us. Pressure grew in my neck, and I struggled to draw a full breath. Before we hit the familiar frozen state of shock, I grabbed onto Kaitlin and pulled her along the walkway up to the broken concrete stairs.

We jumped to the top stoop and inspected the boarding around the door. The edge rattled loosely when I pushed on it and I wrapped my fingers behind it. With little effort, I pulled the board away from the entryway, exposing the massive wooden door behind it. I turned to Kaitlin with wide eyes, and she nodded for me to continue.

I held my breath, certain the board had been screwed on tight last time I tugged on it. Braden had to practically pry my fingers off it when he carried me away from the ward the day before. But now, the board fell away, exposing the original door to the Excited Ward. The one used when patients were first admitted, sending a false sense of regal welcome to the families who were abandoning them there.

I reached for the tarnished brass knob on the solid door and turned it. The bolt within clunked and squeaked against its metal housing. Keeping the knob in my hand, I pushed my body weight against the door, and it moved an inch. The wood seemed to have swelled and was wedged into place firmly. With another heavier shove, I heard the wood creak. The door finally burst open.

The sound of its rusted hinges squealed through the dark foyer, and we turned back to be sure no one saw us entering. Golden light of the setting sun shot vivid beams through tree branches, creating an over-charged feel to the grounds of the asylum. Still seeing no sign of the guys, we stepped into the ward and pushed the door shut behind us, leaving as little evidence as possible that we had entered the condemned building.

Thick must choked me at first, and I rubbed its itch from my eyes. Kaitlin cleared her throat, the sound reverberating through the halls.

"They make it look like a comfortable home from this perspective," Kaitlin commented. "The true horrors are hidden at the far side so no visitors would ever know the truth."

"Exactly," I agreed. The false disguise would put families at ease or helped to get the new arrivals to enter farther within before understanding their grave mistake. And then, it would be too late to turn back.

"Where should we go?" Kaitlin stepped around the rubble piles and rotting, broken furniture.

"Up," I said, glancing toward the decorative stairway at the back of the entryway. "To the patient rooms. Where we saw Emma."

"Shit. I knew you were going to say that." Kaitlin stepped behind me, ready to follow.

"She contacted my father in some way, Kaitlin," I began, as we headed up the creaky stairs. "Like, she was in his head, too. But I think she was ultimately trying to reach me." I thought of Tom's recollection of my dad and all the parts of the story added up.

I whispered the details of what Tom told me by the hanging tree— the part where my dad repeated Emma's name by the same tree he hung himself by, and Kaitlin's pace slowed behind me.

"I don't want to go any farther," she whispered, barely making a sound. "I'm scared, Grace."

We'd already reached the top of the stairs and moved down a decrepit hallway, leading to the cold, institutional section of the ward. Kaitlin stopped moving and turned back.

"Come on, Grace. I want to get out of here. Please." Her voice shook, sending fear through my veins.

"Don't get freaked out, Kaitlin." I fought the fear that threatened to make me follow her. "We just need to see a little more of this place. This one last time."

She glanced down a long corridor similar to the ones we'd been in the day before.

"No." She turned and moved back in the direction we'd come from. "I have to get out of here." Her tone left no room for negotiating, and her firm steps turned into a jog.

I jumped and caught up to her, glancing back over my shoulder at the lost opportunity for exploration, and maybe even answers.

"Damn it, Kaitlin," I said through clenched teeth.

Then she stopped. Looking left, then right, she hesitated on which way to go.

"How do we get out of here?" she barked.

Ignoring her bulging eyes and shallow breathing, I stepped past her to move toward the stairs that led us up here. But the area only opened up into another long corridor. I turned in the opposite direction only to find another endless hallway of debris and peeling paint.

"We must have got turned around somehow." I glanced behind us for any evidence of the wooden railing or archway that led to the stairs to the foyer. But nothing.

"There!' Kaitlin pointed to an opening lined with elaborate wooden molding. "That must be it!" She grabbed my arm, and we hurried toward the passage.

As soon as we reached it, we saw inner boards that sealed the access, and a chipped sign nailed to the blockade.

It read:

Not an Exit

"Shit!" I annunciated every letter of the word.

We turned and jogged through the decaying corridor toward the other end of the ward.

"The caged stairwell with the spray paint must be at this side." Kaitlin bent over, breathing hard. "We can get to the first floor that way."

Our running steps echoed through the hall as we dashed for the way out. Passing door after door, we kept our focus on reaching the stairwell. As we approached, I saw the edge of the anti-suicide caging that filled the stairwell, and relief at its familiarity calmed my rising panic.

Just as we approached the stairwell, we were blocked by more solid boards covering the entire passageway. And another rusted, bent sign filled the middle of the boards and read:

Not an Exit

∼

Kaitlin spun around and grabbed my shoulders. She shook me as if it were my fault we were trapped. Her eyes were wild with terror, and I pushed her arms off me.

"Kaitlin! Stop," I shouted into her face. "Collect yourself and breathe!" I held her eyes with mine until she released her held breath and her shoulders dropped from her ears. "That's better. It won't help us to panic right now. We just need to retrace our steps or find a familiar wing in this place."

Kaitlin focused on inhaling and exhaling as I looked back in the direction we came from. The other end of the long hallway was our only chance.

"Let's move," I commanded, and she followed.

We trekked past the moldy walls and over the piles of trash. Damp, rotting books sat on mounds of squashed brown boxes and bits of old metal shelving. Broken lights hung from unraveling cords in the ceiling, and it felt like the building could collapse on us at any moment.

"I see another stairwell." My voice lifted rejoicefully.

We slowed as we approached the stairs, anxious on what we might find, and my air whooshed from me as I gazed at more boards across the stairs leading down. But a board had fallen away from the stairs leading up, giving us an unexpected opportunity at escape.

"I don't want to go deeper into the ward," Kaitlin whined. "I just want to get out."

"I know, but this looks like our only way out of this part of the building," I said. "We can find another stairway or exit from the upper floor."

We pushed past the fallen boards to enter the caged stairwell. Each step upward created tighter anxiety in my throat and chest. I didn't want to go any farther anymore either. But we had no choice.

We climbed to the next floor, then inspected the metal door that led to the new wing. A faded-yellow window allowed us to see a long stretch of narrow doors inside, along the hallway. They had small cross-shaped windows on them. It looked like the corridor where we'd seen Emma's image.

"I think that's where we were yesterday," I whispered. "Where we saw Emma." I put my hand on the door and tried to open it.

Kaitlin swiped at my arm to stop me. "No! I don't want to go in there." She looked up the stairs behind us. "I want to go higher."

I thought about the exterior of the building. It didn't have that many floors.

"I don't think it goes higher," I said.

"Well, it does." She pointed to the stairs leading up to a confined space with a dark, simple door.

"That must be the attic," I murmured. "There'll be no way out of there."

But that didn't stop her. She was on the stairs and climbing before I could convince her otherwise. After she raced to the top, she pushed on the door with all her weight. It flew open without resistance and she fell inside.

"Slow down, Kaitlin," I yelled, twisting to see behind me to be sure there was no one, or nothing, following us. "You're moving too fast." And I caught up in three jumps, taking two stairs at a time.

The ceiling angled down on both sides, making it impossible to stand anywhere except in the middle of the area. Streams of light crossed each other in every direction, dizzying the effects of the antiques in the space. An old Singer sewing machine and a creepy rocking chair with a shredded seat cushion reigned proudly over the other objects.

Kaitlin stumbled through the junk as if she were lost, struggling to find something she knew. She went straight for a large pile of clothing and fell onto it. Pulling at each garment, she inspected them, all the same, and dug through the pile like there might be something hidden within it.

"What are you doing?" I called to her. "There's no other way out of here." I scoured every corner with my eyes for another exit.

"They're frocks," she said. "The frocks the girls had to wear. They're just like the one Emma had on." Tears filled her eyes as she continued to pull the simple dresses out of the abandoned pile, as if each one was an old friend.

She took one in particular and shook it out. Standing up, she held it against her body and looked down at it. "See, this one with an 'M' embroidered on it, a perfect match. For the girl who's lost her mind."

"What?" I went over to her, pulled the gray frock out of her hands, and snapped, "We're getting out of here now. The floor below us. It's got to have another way out."

I threw the frock back into the pile, and it landed next to one that caught my eye. The ripped pocket. It wouldn't have meant a thing if it hadn't had the large black ink stain on it. The shape of a big spider.

"Fuck." The word fell from my mouth before I could stop it.

Kaitlin followed my gaze and landed on the ink stain.

"Fuck! I knew it," she screamed, covering her face with her hands.

She crumpled to the floor and rocked on her knees, holding her head within her forearms. Her mumbles grew louder as she rocked with wider movement.

She recited numbers incessantly, shooting terror through my entire being. The sound of her voice echoed through the attic adding to my horror.

"235236235236."

∽

The numbers played through my mind like a sickening trick, exploding any final bits of rationality I clung on to.

"235236235…" she repeated, nonstop.

"Stop it," I hollered. "Shut! Up!" I covered my ears with my hands. "I'm getting out of here, whether you're coming or not!"

I turned on my heels and ran for the door. A quick glance back, and I saw Kaitlin scrambling to catch up to me. Thank Christ. Breaking away from her was my only hope at snapping her out of her hysteria.

"Hurry up," I called.

I waited for her to catch up as she stumbled like a drunkard over the junk that littered the floor. As soon as she reached me, I grabbed her hand and flew into the stairwell.

We bombed down the stairs without any effort to stay quiet or go undetected, then smashed through the door to the third-floor wing.

Kaitlin's neurosis returned immediately, and the numbers flew from her mouth again.

"235236235236235236235623…" She repeated the line without pause, even for a breath.

I held her hand tighter, pulling her through the plaster rubble of the long corridor. Her steps fell heavy behind me, and I used all my effort to pull her along.

"She's here," Kaitlin cried out, causing me to stop in my tracks.

"What? Who?" I shouted. "Who, Kaitlin?"

"It's Emma! She's here," she screamed.

My eyes flew wildly around the deteriorating hallway, trailing along the numerous doors that lined each side.

"Don't stop, Kaitlin. We have to get out of here!" I pulled her even harder as my heart nearly pounded out of my chest.

My eyes played tricks on me as every shadow held a looming figure and every alcove proved to have something sinister ready to pull me in.

We ran toward the end of the hall, praying for an open stairwell that would lead us to the first floor. We stumbled through piles of broken ceiling tiles and damp chunks of wall. Without warning, we tripped over the snarled remains of rotting straps. Same as the restraints used in the research building.

Our feet caught in the straps, and we flew in opposite directions. I fell backward into one of the open side doors. Kaitlin spun and landed at the door opposite mine. She scrambled deeper into the confined space, staring at me with wild eyes, and pressed against the far wall.

I pushed myself up to sitting, my eyes darting around my tiny room. Gasping for air, I rushed back out into the hall. Claustrophobia had taken immediate effect, and I rejoiced at my freedom from the narrow space.

Kaitlin continued to push into the back wall of her tiny room. I waved for her to come out, but she shook her head in fear. I pushed the door farther open, in case for some paranormal reason it decided to slam shut on her forever. My imagination had gone haywire now.

As I pressed the door against the outer wall, I looked up at its small window. The cross-shaped opening sent a harrowing chill through me as I considered the subtle torment it would have caused for each patient. My eyes shot down to the end of the hall to land on a crooked white sign with small red letters… **SOLITARY**.

"Holy shit." I exhaled. "Get out of there, Kaitlin. Now!" I reached in for her, too afraid to enter the space for fear of getting trapped in there forever too. "Please!"

Her lips moved with the silent numbers that refused to stop. Somehow, she was able to inch herself closer to me.

Fear bugged her eyes out, and I stretched for her. At last, our fingertips touched, then I grabbed her entire hand and pulled.

I yanked her as hard as I could, tugging her into the hall with me. Wrapping my arm around her shoulder, I pulled her along by my side. Then she stopped again, frozen at the next door. Her gaze stared into the darkness of the small room right next to the one she was just in. Her chin quivered as tears fell from her eyes.

I leaned behind her to see into the small room. Whatever it was she was looking at, it terrified her to the point of immobility.

I lifted my eyes, scared to death of what I might see, and there in the far corner of the small space was a girl. Crouched low, facing into the corner. Her gray frock covered her back and knees, and the ripped pocket held the form of a spider.

"Fuck," I screamed. "Let's get the fuck out of here!" I snatched Kaitlin's shoulders and her head jolted on her neck, snapping her attention to me as I shouted, "Run!"

CHAPTER 20

We flew down the length of the corridor, certain we were being chased by Emma or some other terrifying apparition. Passing each narrow door with cross-shaped windows, rage built within me, thinking of all the girls of the past decades who'd been locked away in solitary to rot. Including Emma.

The vision of her broken, frightened form, hiding in the corner, saddened me to the depth of my core.

"This way," I called to Kaitlin.

A stairway opened up at the end of the hall, and I was determined to use it.

"How do you know which way?" Panic lifted her voice to piercing decibels.

"Trust me! This will lead us out." I left no uncertainty in my tone. And it was easy. I had no doubt this was the way to our freedom. It was our last chance.

Old wooden boards blocked the entrance to the stairs. They'd been nailed across the opening, but several had come loose and fallen. I grabbed onto the biggest one and yanked. With little resistance, it pulled out of the rotted plaster wall and dropped to the ground. It landed on other boards with a smash, drawing my attention to the mangled sign beneath it. The words '**Not an Exit**' peeked out from the pile, and I kicked at it with frustration.

I reached for Kaitlin. Just as I moved toward the first step, a harrowing sound echoed through the corridor behind us. It could have been the wind. Maybe even creaking boards. But it sounded like an older woman's voice commanding us to stop.

The terrifying sound froze my muscles, and I stared in the direction it came from.

"You will stop at once!" The harsh voice filled the air around us with a chill that shot straight into my heart.

Kaitlin's face contorted with sheer terror and she pushed past me, nearly falling down the stairs.

"What the fuck?" she screamed as her feet hammered on the stairs in panicked flight.

I raced after her, flying down the steps away from the haunting sound of the old woman. I caught up to Kaitlin and pushed on her shoulders to make her move faster, certain the evil woman was about to grab me and never let go.

Her brazen voice crashed into the stairwell. "Stop at once! Or you'll remain in the hole for another week!"

My muscles nearly liquefied as her threat generated fear in me that scattered my brain to the wind.

"Shit! Hurry up." I shoved Kaitlin down the final steps leading to the first floor. "Out here!"

I shot through the heavy metal door into the darkness of the first floor. The boarded-up windows let in a small bit of light, but I followed my instinct toward the center of the building. We ran without stopping, glancing over our shoulders every second, screaming at every strange object.

A carved-wood railing came into view. The stairs of the foyer...

"That's it," I screamed in relief. "The front door!"

Tears filled my eyes as I pulled on the knob. The door resisted, caught again in its swollen wooden frame. I looked back to Kaitlin, only to see tears pouring from her eyes, too—her terror causing her to pace while searching wildly for her hidden assailant.

"My hands are too sweaty," I yelled. "I can't get a grip on it."

"What the fuck?" she screamed. "Get us out of here!" Her voice filled the foyer with a screech that came from deep within her.

I rubbed my hands on my pants. With one more turn and pull, the door inched toward me. I rubbed again, then heaved with all my might. With great resistance, the door finally groaned open, as if reluctant to let us out.

Kaitlin pushed at my back, trying to get us out as quickly as possible.

"Go, go, go." She shuffled behind me to extract herself faster from the confines of the ward.

We fell out onto the stoop and jumped down the concrete steps. The sound of the heavy wooden door slamming behind us sent a new level of hysteria through us.

We tore across the lawn around to the side of the building. The quickest exit from the grounds of the asylum was our only focus.

I glanced toward the chapel and the research building, at first blinded by the golden rays of the setting sun shooting through the tree branches. Confusion twisted my already-fried brain as I realized the sun was at the exact same position it had been in when we entered the ward. I turned back to Kaitlin, but she was already making distance toward the woods at the back of the building.

"Kaitlin, wait for me," I yelled, turning to the other buildings one more time, in search of our friends.

There, at the edge of the research lab, I caught a glimpse of the guys, although Tom was nowhere to be seen. They were looking all around, searching for us. I couldn't see well enough through my blurred, teary vision, but it seemed like Braden saw me.

The high walls of the Excited Ward loomed over us, and its dark shadows reached out as if trying to recapture me. Adrenaline shot through my legs and I ran faster than ever before, catching up to Kaitlin.

Running was our only chance at getting away from the sinister hold of the ward.

Tripping over branches and rotting leaves, we followed a trail into the thick trees that surrounded the asylum. Our frantic breathing filled the air around us as we searched for an opening in the woods that would lead us to safety.

As we went deeper into the cover of the trees, I slowed my frantic pace enough to draw a full breath.

"Slow down, Kaitlin," I called. "We're okay now. Nothing's following us."

"We're not far enough yet." She kept pushing deeper into the woods. "I can still feel it."

I chased after her, knowing she wasn't wrong. I felt it, too. No matter how far we ran, it was still right there.

Then she finally slowed her pace and I had a chance to catch up. Her gaze remained ahead of her, but her sprint had slowed to a steady walk. A moment later, she came to an abrupt stop and remained, unflinching, in her place. She turned back to me and called out.

"I see something."

∽

I caught up to Kaitlin to see what she had found. Black, wrought-iron fencing. Rotting and falling in. My eyes trailed along the length of the fence and it lined the edge of the trees. Within its border was an open field of lush grass and gently rolling slopes.

"This way." I moved along the fence, searching for an opening.

Pushing branches away and snapping twigs under our feet, we made our way along the perimeter.

"I'm still scared, Grace," Kaitlin whispered. "My head won't stop spinning."

"I know. Me too." I stumbled on a branch, forcing my way through the brush. "I don't understand what's been happening."

I gazed into the open field, cursing the difficulty of finding an entrance into its sanctuary.

"We saw her again." She choked back the words and then swallowed hard. "She's still in there."

"Ya." My head shook in disbelief. "I can't think about that right now. I just need to know this is over. I can't do this anymore."

Getting lost in the ward, no, trapped, and then seeing Emma again... my mind was frantic with the insanity of it all. But it was the old woman's voice, cold and cruel, that truly terrified me. Shouting at us to stop at once. The sound of the words in my mind shot despair through me again. She somehow had gotten a hold of my soul back in the ward and I feared she'd never let it go.

"Do you think Emma's trapped in limbo or something?" Kaitlin mumbled, as if lost in thought. "I can't help but feel bad for her. Like, she's no different from us. I feel like, she was probably a lot of fun."

I slowed my steps, gripping onto one of the spiky posts of the fence.

"Maybe." I slowed to examine Kaitlin.

It was the first time in a while she'd said something aside from wanting to go home. She'd tapped into something new that I hadn't considered before, and it felt right. Emma wasn't scary. She was like us.

And her being trapped in limbo wasn't that far-fetched. She'd died wrongfully. She'd been held prisoner against her will. A tormented soul.

I finally saw where the fencing turned.

"There. It's the edge of the fence." I hurried along again, hoping to find a road or some way out of the woods.

We jogged along the rusted fencing and reached the corner. Pushing overgrowth back, we pressed around it and a gate came into view. It opened into the field and didn't appear to be chained or locked in any way.

As we got closer, it became clear that the gate was collapsing from age. Ivy covered its decorative metal scrolls and at the top, a plaque was screwed into the middle. It appeared familiar to me, and I stepped closer for a better look.

I twisted to check behind us and there, beyond the evergreens, a road revealed itself just over a ridge. Train tracks cut across it farther up, and I recognized it as the same road to the asylum that we'd driven many times. And I'd seen this exact gate from out the car window and dismissed it as a random sight.

My breath released and fell out of me. I knew where we were. We were safe.

I turned back to Kaitlin and sucked my breath in again. She hunched over, shaking in front of the gate with her eyes glued to the plaque.

"What?" I called. "What is it?"

She didn't move and just kept staring at it.

I stepped up next to her and looked at the sign. It was a dedication, like a memorial. I glanced into her face wondering what had shocked her and it remained frozen, unblinking.

"Kaitlin?" I whispered.

I turned back and read the plaque.

In dedication to Dr. Thomas Johnson
Superintendent of Blackwood Asylum 1896-1936
For your selfless service to these souls so they may never be forgotten
"For we too have lived, loved, and laughed."

"What the fuck?" I whispered. "Dr. Thomas Johnson? What the actual fuck?" I couldn't form enough words to express my inner freak out. "Tom Johnson? What? Is he a fucking ghost?"

Kaitlin continued to stare at the sign, then finally lifted her eyes and looked past the border of the wrought-iron fencing, out across the green field. Her voice moved from deep within her without any emotion or affect as she stated, "It's the lost cemetery."

∽

I moved past Kaitlin in silence to push the rusted, bent gate further open. Squeezing through, I gazed across the rolling field, wondering where all the headstones could be.

Kaitlin remained frozen at first, but then lifted her eyes to meet mine. A lost look of confusion settled deep within her gaze and her shoulders slumped. Slowly, her feet shuffled and then she began to walk toward me.

We entered the graveyard as the sun made its final dip below the tree line. Twilight's glow sent an ethereal feel throughout the grounds, and we moved farther into the moss-covered clearing. A gentle breeze brushed along my ears, and I thought I might have heard Braden's voice calling my name.

"I don't like it here," Kaitlin whimpered. "Something's not right."

I looked around for any sign of danger, only to see gentle slopes of lush green grass and spongy moss.

"It's like it vanished," I mumbled. "Like it never actually existed."

Kaitlin glanced up at me with worry as her chin trembled.

Moving toward the center of the clearing, I surveyed the entire space confined within the black fencing. There was nothing to be found.

Then, taking another step, I stumbled on the edge of a hidden rock, buried in the long grass. I steadied myself and looked down at where I'd tripped. An indentation in the ground held the chunk of moss I'd kicked up.

I stepped away to examine the depression more closely. Then I noticed there was another identical impression in the moss right next to it. As I pulled back, more indentations came into my view. Rows and rows, covering the entire field with thousands of pockmarks.

My eyes widened as I gasped and dropped to my knees. I pulled the moss away from the slight impression in the ground, uncovering the side of a stone marker. I ran my fingers around its edges as I pulled more moss away. The marker was about the size of my hands held side by side.

"There are more," I said to Kaitlin, pointing to the next one in the row. "Look."

She dropped to her knees, pulling the moss away from the next stone marker.

We brushed at the surfaces, removing dirt and debris.

"There are markings," I said as my fingers traced weathered engraving in the stone.

We brushed and blew at the surfaces again, exposing shapes.

"I see numbers," I called out.

"Me too," Kaitlin said, blowing at the dirt with short, shallow breaths.

My finger traced along the eroded carvings and I read aloud, "236."

Kaitlin read hers at the same time. "235."

The numbers echoed in the air around us, repeating themselves over and over in my mind. Their familiarity awakened every last nerve as I searched for their meaning.

"235236235236." Kaitlin's voice brought my attention back as she chanted the string of numbers without end.

"Stop it, Kaitlin!" I covered my ears and stepped away, only to trip on another stone just below the number marker. "What the fuck?" I cried in disoriented frustration.

I dropped again, then pulled the moss off the larger hidden stone. I exposed the shiny edges right away. Newer, polished granite, like the stones used for modern grave markers, probably installed more recently.

"Kaitlin, search," I commanded. "Uncover the other stone!"

The moss pulled away in one clean slab, exposing the precise machine-cut carvings. I brushed away the dirt, then stood back in horror.

Kaitlin jumped up at the same time, whimpering.

A scream grew in my throat as I stared at the stone. "No. No. No." The words purged out of me as I grabbed my hair in terror.

As Kaitlin comprehended the situation, her screams met mine. We reached for each other in a desperate embrace.

As we stared down at the stones, we read the horrifying truth of our situation.

Grace Frances Parker
1902-1920

Kaitlin 'Missy' Edwards
1901-1920

We dropped to our knees with inconsolable screams.

A gateway to our pasts had been opened in our brains, and there was nothing we could do to close it. We'd seen glimpses of it—in the ward, at the tree, and now the truth lay in the ground beneath our feet.

Trapped in limbo. Forgotten. Lost forever in the asylum.

I tore at the moss on the stone next to mine, knowing exactly what I would find.

I ripped at it, exposing the shiny granite marker.

Emma Grangley
1902-1920

My vision narrowed to a pinpoint of focus as my brain allowed the window to a past life to remain open. I pressed at my head to close the gaping portal, to end the crazy dream that was my reality.

Kaitlin fought it, too. She crouched onto her knees, rocking and screaming, calling out the numbers over and over.

"235236237235236237."

237 was a new part of the sequence. I kicked at Emma's old stone marker, exposing the corroded numbers on it.

237.

In a flash, my mind traveled back to the ward. To the corridor with rows of narrow doors. I was back in the small room with the cross-shaped window. The room I'd fallen into earlier. But this time, the door was closed, and I was trapped within it.

I leapt to the window, then pressed my hands onto the cross-shape and pulled my face to it. Staring out in bewilderment, I looked into the hall at the room across from mine. In an instant, hands reached into the other cross-shaped window and a face appeared in it. Kaitlin's.

I looked over her door, gaping at the number plaque just above it.

At the same time, her eyes lifted above my door. Horror washed over her face.

Her room number was listed on the plaque. 235.

My eyes jumped to the door next to hers. The number was 237. Emma's. And in an instant, I knew mine had to be 236.

And that was how I would forever be remembered. Patient number 236. No name. No family. Just a number. My heart plummeted from my chest as I fought the truth of my existence. The existence that left me wandering, searching for rescue from the ward.

"Let me out of here," I screamed with every ounce of strength I had. "I don't belong here! Let me out!"

Kaitlin's shrieks matched mine as we shook on our doors in sheer terror.

How could they do this to us? How was there no one who could help us? We were held prisoner, trapped within the ward. And there was no way out.

"Help me, Grace," Kaitlin screamed. "Get me out of here. We don't belong here. They'll be coming for us soon!"

Her words silenced me for a moment. It was true, they'd be coming.

Then my screams grew louder and more hysterical as I feared for what was to become of us. Emma's door was slightly open. She wasn't in isolation anymore. They'd already come for her.

And we were next.

My screams mixed with Kaitlin's into a frenzy of mind-shattering panic.

"You will stop at once." The sound of an older woman's voice filled the corridor with its brazen tone.

I jolted toward the sound to see an angry woman in an old-fashioned nurse's outfit stomping down the corridor with a glowing lantern in her hand. A port-wine stain blotched her forehead, and her narrow eyes held empty disdain.

"You will stop at once," she repeated. "Or be sent to the hole in restraints for another week."

Her evil voice drowned out in the depths of the corridor from the insane sound of our desperate screams.

EPILOGUE

My arms dragged down with the weight of restraints, and I pulled to break free. Weakness moved through my veins like morphine, and I stopped struggling against its soothing calm.

Braden's voice echoed in the back of my mind, making me smile at its familiar tone.

"I don't know," he stated to someone unknown as the sound of a siren filled the air. "I just found them like that in the field, screaming." He paused, seeming to gather his thoughts. "They were inconsolable. Just screaming." Fear crept out of his voice as he struggled to keep the shake steady.

The cemetery!

It all flooded back into my fogged awareness.

"Where's Kaitlin?" The words bounced through my mind, but I couldn't get them to leave my mouth.

Where was she?

Where was I?

I pulled on my restraints again as fear crept through me like an evil demon.

"They were afraid of something." Braden's voice broke through again. "Something that had been…chasing them. Hunting them." His volume trailed off into near silence.

He leaned in closer to me. I opened my eyes as much as possible, to narrow slits. Light poured in, blinding me. Flashing red and blue lights. Medical equipment all around.

"Grace," he whispered. "You're safe now."

I pulled on the familiar restraints one more time.

And then I whispered, "Am I?"

The End.

Don't miss the sample chapters of Book Two, *The Excited Ward*, at the end of this novel.

AFTERWORD

I hope you enjoyed Book One of the Asylum Savant Series, The Shuttered Ward.

Be sure to check out the sample chapters of Book Two, The Excited Ward, at the end of this novel.

Also, visit my website for more information about this series and my other books.

Thank you!

www.jenniferrosemcmahon.com
To sign up for my newsletter:
https://www.subscribepage.com/f1p9w6

ALSO BY JENNIFER ROSE MCMAHON

PIRATE QUEEN SERIES
Bohermore, Book One
Inish Clare, Book Two
Ballycroy, Book Three
Rockfleet, Novella (Book 2.5)

IRISH MYSTIC LEGENDS SERIES
Legend Hunter, Book One
Curse Raider, Book Two
Truth Seer, Book Three

ASYLUM SAVANT SERIES
The Shuttered Ward, Book One
The Excited Ward, Book Two
The Forgotten Ward, Book Three

ACKNOWLEDGMENTS

A huge thank you to my urban explorer partner and eldest son, Rory McMahon. For your enthusiasm for this story to be told and the adventurous research that brought it to life in a way that never would have been possible without your help. Thank you, me boy, for the camaraderie, support, and love.

Thank you to Cynthia Shepp for her amazing editing super powers and for meeting tight deadlines while juggling preparations for her wedding.

Thank you to Rebecca Frank, designer goddess, for her fabulous book covers.

A very special thank you to my amazing beta-readers. Several high school students joined my book club to review the manuscript for The Shuttered Ward. With red pens in hand, they critiqued the pages like masters and kept my prose relevant. They were also never shy in writing "awk" in any area that sounded or felt awkward. Thank you so much to Abby Gordon, Alicia Dean, Mei Kawabe, Maddie Klepper, Samira Kerkach, and Rebecca DeBenedictis.

And lastly, to John Thompson, Chair of the Medfield State Hospital Building and Grounds Committee, for sharing the history of the institution and providing a top-notch tour around the grounds. Many of your stories are woven into this book and I hope you can find them all. Thank you so much for your warm welcome, and your generosity of time and knowledge.

ABOUT THE AUTHOR

Jennifer Rose McMahon is a USA Today Bestselling Author who has been creating her Pirate Queen series, Irish Mystic Legends series, and Asylum Savants series since her college days abroad in Ireland. Her passion for Irish legends, ancient cemeteries, medieval ghost stories, and abandoned asylums has fueled her adventurous story telling, while her husband's decadent brogue carries her imagination through the centuries. When she's not in her own world writing about castles and curses, she can be found near Boston in the local coffee shop, yoga studio, or at the beach…most often answering to the name 'Mom' by her fab children four.

For more information
www.jenniferrosemcmahon.com
info@jenniferrosemcmahon.com

SAMPLE CHAPTERS OF BOOK TWO, THE EXCITED WARD

THE EXCITED WARD
Book Two, Asylum Savants Series

CHAPTER ONE

The sound of my shallow breathing filled the darkness and grew louder as I pulled on my restraints. Pain shot up my arms causing me to wince. Whatever it was that had made them think tying me down was necessary, it couldn't have been that bad. Even if I *had* lost my mind at the cemetery--screaming my head off, that still wouldn't be enough to justify this level of barbaric treatment. I swore to myself I'd sue their asses once I was released.

I tugged at my wrist again and hissed in pain. My skin burned like fire from the friction and I wiggled my legs instead. My ankles screamed out with the same raw sting causing me to jump. But my shoulders lifted only a few inches before I fell back down from the pressure of more restraints. One push of my hips confirmed they were strapped down too.

My heart rate shot to full panic as I searched through the echoing darkness.

"Kaitlin? Are you there?" My hushed voice bounced through the room and a rustle came from the far side.

"Grace?" Her voice scratched out of her.

"Shit, Kaitlin. Where are we?" I whispered. "No lights or monitors? Is this some form of concussion therapy or something?" I stared into the blackness listening for sounds of nurses in the hallway.

She rustled more and whimpered in the cold shadows. "I can't move. I'm strapped to the bed."

"I know. Me too." My dry voice cracked. "All I remember is the flashing lights of the ambulance. And Braden's face. But that's all. They must have drugged us when we got here, to calm us down."

"My wrists are sticky," she murmured. "They burn. I think my straps are too tight. They're cutting into me."

How could they have not noticed the restraints were hurting us? Our wrists and ankles were injured from the abrasive ties. Someone was going to be in a lot of trouble for neglecting us when we clearly needed a much higher level of attention and care.

It was all to blame on our heads, no doubt. Our concussions. We'd pushed ourselves too far, to the point of needing to be re-admitted to the hospital. Again. Unfortunately, this time, it probably looked pretty bad. I was sure Braden had told the medics everything he saw at the asylum and from what I could remember, it included a lot of running and screaming.

I squeezed my eyes shut to remember more and pictured the abandoned asylum. Before the ambulance came, Kaitlin and I had just escaped from the boarded-up Excited Ward. It had tried to keep us lost inside its walls but we were finally able to break out.

My head hurt from the effort of conjuring the memory. There was hysteria, but it was in the moment when we found the hidden cemetery that it all came crushing down on us.

Flashes of the grave markers burst through my mind, reminding me of the most frightening moment of my life--the vision of my own death.

SAMPLE CHAPTERS OF BOOK TWO, THE EXCITED WARD

I sucked in a gulp of air, remembering the terror that ripped at my soul as I saw my full name on the gravestone. Kaitlin's too. And then Emma's. We were all there beneath my feet. Together.

Poor Braden. I thought back to the lost expression on his face. He'd probably assumed I'd officially lost my mind. And in that moment, I had.

But I was thinking with clarity now. Too many coincidences had lined up, making the events seem like more than they were. Like they were real.

I wouldn't go back to the abandoned asylum now, I vowed. It was too volatile. It held too much energy somehow, like it was haunted. Or evil. Almost like it wouldn't let us go.

"I don't want to go back there, Kaitlin. Ever," I whispered as a tear fell from my eye and trickled into my ear.

Then a stream of tears rolled from my eyes and pooled in my ears as I thought more about the crazy events at the asylum and the situation that I now found myself in. The tears made me itch. I shook my head to help dry them but the itch only intensified. There was nothing I could do. I couldn't reach up.

"Fuck." I twitched on my cold metal bed. "What the fuck is going on? Nurse!" I called out. "Nurse. We're awake. We need help."

I waited for a response--footsteps, beepers, lights. Anything.

Kaitlin whimpered in her bed.

"Nurse! Help us!" I yelled louder.

Finally, the sound of hard heels clomping down steps filled the space, then moved closer to the door.

"You will stop at once!" The brazen sound of an older woman's voice blasted through the door. "Or you'll remain in the hole for another week!"

#

My body stiffened from the cruelty in her tone. The familiar, harsh stabbing of her voice smothered my hopes that everything would be okay. And then, there was no mistake, everything was absolutely not okay.

I held my breath until her footsteps moved away from the door and clomped back up the stairs.

"Kaitlin?" I whimpered.

But there was no answer. Only quiet sounds of crying.

"It's okay, Kaitlin. It's not real." My voice shook from the shock of hearing the woman's threat.

I didn't need to see the woman to know there was a mark of a port-wine stain on her forehead. I'd seen her before, in the flashbacks from the boarded-up ward when we were trapped inside. Her old-fashioned nurse's cap and the glow of her rattling lantern next to her face taunted me. She'd hunted us in the Excited Ward and tormented us with those exact same words.

"We're sleeping," I whispered. "They must have sedated us to help our brains heal. The darkness and the silence help too."

I convinced myself of our safety with my reassuring words to Kaitlin. I'd heard of this before, induced coma. It sounded like a big deal, but honestly, in our condition at the cemetery, I wouldn't blame them for knocking us out for a while.

My body shook from the damp cold as I watched shapes in the room begin to take form. Dull light entered through a narrow window high up on the back wall, allowing me to see shadows of details in the room. Dawn's light grew brighter by the minute and I blinked as my eyes adjusted.

At first, I noticed the shape of the door and medical equipment by our beds. The silent monitors must have been specialized for our symptoms, with no beeping and no lights. I was grateful for the high-tech instruments but still needed to understand why we were restrained to such a high degree. Embarrassment washed over me as I considered what the medical staff must have thought when we'd first arrived—as if we were a threat to ourselves or others.

"Kaitlin, the sun's rising," I said. "We're going to be okay. Just hang on while your brain clears of whatever meds they gave us."

Her choppy breathing and sniffles were her only response. Poor Kaitlin. She was terrified by our predicament.

As the morning light grew brighter, scattered streams of illumination zig-zagged through the small lead-glass window, sending dusty beams throughout the room. The walls remained dark though and the objects within held their shadowy form. I had expected bright white and sterile stainless steel of a hospital room and squeezed my eyes shut to reset my vision.

"Please. Please. Please," I whispered to myself.

Please be normal when I open my eyes.

I snuck one eye open first, then the other burst wide and I stared all around the room. Damp stone walls surrounded us, dripping with moisture that ran toward a dirt floor. I gasped in horror at the unsanitary conditions and my gaze darted toward the door. Its heavy wooden features assaulted my senses with rusted iron hardware and lack of any window to see out.

Frozen from fear, my head refused to move as I forced my eyes sideways to look at Kaitlin. Trailing across the room, my vision fell on one of the machines between us. Instead of a device displaying heart rates and respiration, it was an old wooden table that held a metal tray of large needles protruding from glass vials and other old-fashioned medical supplies from at least a hundred years ago. A stack of large metal bowls sat on the ground leaning on one of the legs of the table.

"What the fuck?" My voice caught in my throat as my eyes jumped to Kaitlin.

She stared at me with wild-eyes as if they were about to bug out of her head. Her cheeks were sunken in and dark circles shadowed her eyes. Her grey hospital gown had blood stains on it from the wounds on her wrists. Her restraints had cut her up bad and her ankles showed the same level of injury.

My breath turned to panting as panic rose in me. I turned my attention to my own condition and jolted on my hard metal bed as my mind processed my own bloody wrists and ankles.

"Grace." Kaitlin's voice whispered to me.

I turned back to her with horror plastered across my face. I couldn't hide my terror from her any longer.

"Kaitlin?"

She moved her hand and her fingers grabbed onto the edge of her gray hospital gown. She tugged on the rough fabric and then shot a sickening smirk at me.

"Grace. It's my frock. The one with the 'M' on it."

CHAPTER TWO

I stared in horror at Kaitlin's gray frock and then glanced at my own. Screams threatened to tear out of me and I stifled them with what was left of my inner strength.

It all had to still be a dream. A nightmare.

I remembered being taken by ambulance. With Braden by my side. But where was he now? Where was my mother? Where were Kaitlin's parents?

We were alone.

I prayed silently to be rescued from the insanity of my dream. To wake up and be normal again. But my grip on the details of what I hoped for started to fade. I struggled to keep Braden's face fresh in my mind, but he blurred and blended into a sea of faces that became strangers.

It began to feel like what I had been hoping for, the reality I craved, was the actual dream. This, here and now, was my new reality.

"Kaitlin. What happened?" I whispered. "How did we get here?"

Her eyes remained fixed on me, unblinking.

"We shouldn't have tried to escape again," she murmured. "It's impossible to escape this place."

Her words caused my focus to narrow into a fine point of clear sight and understanding washed over me.

We were patients here.

Trapped against our wills.

Prisoners within the Excited Ward of the Blackwood Insane Asylum.

"Do you remember everything?" I asked. "Do you remember the..." I thought hard to recall the details of my memory. "The..."

"I remember screaming," she said. "I remember running. And..." She strained to find words.

We had both lost hold of the events that landed us in this place. I glanced at the tray of needles and would do anything to ensure they didn't administer any more of whatever had been in them.

Obedience.

That was what they sought.

Compliance.

It was all they wanted in a place like this and so we would have to give it to them.

"We need to do whatever they say," I whispered. "If we fight, they'll give us more of that medicine."

She nodded with choppy motion.

"Don't even complain about the straps," I added. "We can take care of our wounds ourselves. We just need to get out of here before we die of hypothermia or starvation." I paused and listened beyond our door. "We just need to be patient. And wait."

Kaitlin rustled on her bed, shifting her hips to the side. I felt it too, the ache in my bones from the hard surface of the cold slabs we laid on.

She turned her head toward me again and in a low tone, barely audible, she asked, "Where's Emma?"

#

Kaitlin's words exploded my mind into shattered pieces that scattered out of my reach. Hearing Emma's name evoked a level of emotion I couldn't contain. Fear and desperation burst out of me in a flood of tears with loud gasps for life-saving air. The sound of my erratic breathing filled the room, escalating the tension to heights of sheer panic.

"Water therapy?" I squeaked.

I dared say the words for fear of making them true. Could they have sent Emma for more water therapy?

"I hope the hell not," Kaitlin answered. "She barely survived the last time they tried to drown her."

Jesus. Emma always got the worst of it. Nurse Totten hated her for some reason. Her spirit. Her intelligence. Her beauty. Those natural blessings all worked against her in this place.

"Nurse Totten." I spoke her name out loud with a shudder.

I was sure she was the one who shouted at us through the door. And she was the one who would have tortured Emma too. She had no soul. Her empty eyes held only vacant hate. Someone had hurt her at some point and she was determined to get vengeance on those weaker than her.

"You mean Nurse Rotten," Kaitlin murmured. "Her birthmark gets brighter any time she gets mad. Its shade is the perfect measure for how much trouble you're going to be in." Her weak smirk pulled up one side of her face. "So do we just wait for her to come back for us?"

I thought about our other options. We could find a way to unfasten the straps, push our beds to the small window, and break out of it somehow. But then what? I was still disoriented. Probably drugged. We could get lost and then caught. Our punishment would be even worse the next time, I was sure. Worse like Emma's.

"I think we just wait," I said. "It's the only way to get to Emma. If we run now, it would be like leaving her to the wolves."

"You're right." She dropped her head back onto the metal slab with a bang. "How did we even get caught? I can't remember any of what happened."

No matter how hard I searched my memory, I couldn't find the pieces of what happened either. Whatever drug they gave us, it had caused full-blown amnesia. It was like we had brain damage or something.

"I'm not even sure what happened before all of this," I groaned. "Like, how did we get sent to a madhouse in the first place?" My entire existence was a blur and I stared at the needles and vials on the tray,

SAMPLE CHAPTERS OF BOOK TWO, THE EXCITED WARD

as if they were to blame. "But at least I still feel smart. Like I know I can out-think Totten. I know we can figure a way out of here. We just need to be clever and keep our whits about us."

The calculating clarity in my brain gave me the confidence that we wouldn't rot in here. I believed deep within my soul we had what it took to get out. We just needed the chance.

"How do we outsmart them when they're the ones with the keys and the power?"

"We'll trick them," I stated. "We need to act scared. And submissive. Like their punishment worked and we're ready to be compliant. That's all they want. They just want us to be mindless zombies."

Kaitlin drew in a deep breath. "Okay. But how the hell will we convince Emma to do it too? She's way too headstrong and outspoken."

"I know," I chuckled.

Just thinking of Emma's antics made me laugh. She never put up with anyone's bull and was ready at all times for whatever confrontation was ahead of her. It was her downfall though, in a place like this. She was truly doomed from the moment she set foot here.

"Wait," Kaitlin shushed me. "I hear someone coming."

#

My heart jumped into my throat as I listened with every fiber of my being. Kaitlin was right. Someone was moving around outside of our door, maybe more than one person.

I gathered my composure, preparing for whoever might walk through our door, and no matter how hard I tried, I still nearly lost continence from the terror.

I turned to Kaitlin and whispered without barely making a sound. She stared at my mouth, reading my lips while straining to hear me.

"We need to be compliant. Be agreeable to whatever they ask us to do. No matter how embarrassing or shameful it may be."

She nodded her head.

I continued, "They will violate us. They'll treat us like animals. But we have to be grateful for their kindness. Do you understand?"

Kaitlin gulped as if trying to swallow a basketball. Then nodded her head again.

Before I could say anything else, the door smashed open with a crash.

Nurse Totten stormed in first, followed by a smaller-framed nursemaid who peered at us from behind her. Light poured into the room from the hall and I squinted my eyes against its assault.

"What a shame. Light too bright?" Nurse Totten chided me.

My first instinct was to sneer at her and roll my eyes, but instead, I averted my gaze to avoid confrontation and kept a solemn expression on my face.

She turned to the nursemaid behind her. "Unfasten the restraints. They'll need to relieve themselves." Her callous voice cut into my flesh like the crack of a whip.

The meek nursemaid came to my bed first and fumbled with the straps. Her eyes met mine as she loosened them from my bloody wrists and a flash of pity escaped her gaze before she could shield it.

I allowed my freed wrists to remain at my sides even though the urge to rub them and move my arms was at the point of unbearable.

She removed all of the other restraints that held my body to the metal slab and I nearly lept out of my skin as the joy of freedom coursed through me. Instead though, I remained still and barely moved a muscle.

The nursemaid shifted to Kaitlin next and I kept watch of Nurse Totten from the corner of my eye. She stared at me, assessing my condition and hesitated like she wasn't sure what to do next.

"Up for yer piss," she barked as she kicked a metal pan across the floor toward my bed.

I sat up and quickly hopped off the metal table while keeping my eyes off the purple mark that throbbed on her head. My knees wobbled beneath me and I held the edge of the bed for stability. Shivers quaked through my entire body as I positioned myself over the pan.

SAMPLE CHAPTERS OF BOOK TWO, THE EXCITED WARD

My shy-pee was going to be put the test under these circumstances and I grimaced as my bladder muscles tightened like a vice. Squatting, I hovered over the pan while holding the fabric of my frock up around me. Under Nurse Totten's stern glare, I was certain I wouldn't produce a drop but fortunately, my attention shifted to Kaitlin. The horrified expression painted across her face sent a jolt of laughter through me.

Her eyes nearly fell out of her head at the sight of me hovering over the pan and then, in my efforts to stifle my laughter, my pee released. I hid my reddening face in my chest in hopes they would think I was crying instead of laughing. And all I could think about was how I was going to kill Kaitlin for hitting my funny bone at the worst possible time, yet again.

As soon as I was able, I lifted my face and finished up. I dreaded Kaitlin having to go through the same humiliating process as Nurse Totten kicked a pan toward her next.

"I'm sure you'll enjoy your breakfast," she said as she gestured for the nursemaid to bring in the tray.

Now was my chance to take attention off Kaitlin so she could do her business with a little privacy.

"Yes. Thank you," I said in a low tone with my eyes locked to the floor. "Where should I bring this?" I asked, reaching for my filled bedpan.

Nurse Totten stood taller with her shoulders squared. "Bring it to Agnes. She'll show you what to do with it." She glanced at my bloodied hands and feet, then looked away in disgust.

I lifted my pan carefully, taking small steps with it, not only to avoid sloshing, but to allow time for Kaitlin to finish up and follow me. Agnes had us spill the contents into a large vessel on her cart and then we went back into our room without any argument or hesitation.

I climbed back onto my bed and signaled for Kaitlin to do the same. With a few adjustments, I prepared myself to be restrained again.

"Eat yer breakfast first," Nurse Totten barked.

SAMPLE CHAPTERS OF BOOK TWO, THE EXCITED WARD

"Thank you," I said and reached for the tin bowl of curdled porridge.

Kaitlin followed my lead and we ate the cold, clumpy mush like it was a stack of hot, syrupy pancakes. In a few gulps, we were scraping the bottoms clean.

"Thank you," Kaitlin murmured.

"Speak up, Missy." Nurse Totten grumbled. "No mumbling."

"Thank you," Kaitlin said with more power. "Thank you for the nice breakfast."

Her eyes dropped and the last syllable nearly choked her, but I was proud of her. She was doing great.

We both adjusted ourselves back on our beds, waiting to be restrained again.

Nurse Totten paced, as if deciding what to do. Then, after what felt like an eternity, she stepped out the door and called out.

"They're ready to come up," she shouted.

CHAPTER THREE

Keeping silent, I stared at Kaitlin in exhilaration. We were being released from The Hole. There was no telling how long we'd been in there but the weakness in my legs proved it was at least several days, if not more.

"Don't speak of it with the other girls," Totten growled. "Not a mention or you'll find yourselves back in here for a longer stint. Agnes will see that you get cleaned up before you re-enter the ward." She clomped her way along the damp hall, adjusting her small white cap, as she led us to a set of dark, stone stairs.

At the top of the stairs was a sealed wooden door. We were in the basement of our ward--'The Hole', as it was so appropriately named. No one could hear us down here. We were simply forgotten.

Nurse Totten pushed on the door at the top of the steps and loosened its seal, then turned back to us. "Have no mind of trying to run away again. We won't stand having you giving the other girls notions of what might exist out of these walls. It only causes anxiety and upset to their structured time here." She pushed on the door one final time and it groaned open. "Consequences for disturbing the order of the asylum can be severe."

Agnes followed us, carrying the tray from breakfast. She avoided eye contact at all cost and it exposed her vulnerability. It was clear she was new here, a nurse-in-training maybe, and her heart hadn't turned to stone yet. At least there were still a *few* humans left in this place.

Nurse Totten ushered us along a back hallway on the first floor and led us into a small room with Agnes. A barrel sat in the middle of the room, filled with water.

"Get them cleaned up and then back into their hall," Nurse Totten ordered Agnes. "No delay." Then she turned and rattled her hard heels down the corridor.

Kaitlin and I moved to the barrel in an instant, dying to wash the dried blood and filth from our bodies and our hair. We whipped off our frocks and I lifted my toe in first. My foot retracted as if being electrocuted, as the water was freezing.

My eyes darted to Kaitlin's and she pressed her lips together in resignation. I stepped into the freezing water and she followed. Ladles and old bars of soap sat on a bench next to the barrel and we wasted no time pouring gray water over ourselves. Our bodies shuddered from the cold but we moved quickly, finding joy in the simplicity of getting clean.

Agnes handed us ripped towels that felt like they must have once been sheets and we did our best to dry off with them. I bent over and wrapped the fabric around my hair and then flipped it back like a turban. Agnes stared at me like she'd never seen such a thing before and I nearly laughed at her confused expression.

Kaitlin watched Agnes' reaction and let out a small snort from holding back her own laughter and I nearly lost it. My shoulders shook and I used all my mental power to think of something else, something sad, so I wouldn't burst out laughing.

It was crazy. Even in a place like this, Kaitlin and I were connected so deeply that we could still find humor under such oppressive conditions.

"Okay, come on." Agnes urged us. "Up to your rooms."

We followed her through the white-washed halls and up a flight of stairs. She pushed through a heavy metal door and walked with us down a long corridor.

"You're to be separated now," she said. "Each with a different room. Nurse Totten's orders."

My eyes darted to Kaitlin's. We couldn't be separated. We needed as much time together as possible to conspire our escape. But challenging Nurse Totten's orders was the last thing we could do at this point.

"You're here." Agnes pointed me to my room. "And you're there." She aimed her hand to the room across the hall for Kaitlin. "Now, do as you're told and there shouldn't be any trouble."

Her words were a warning to us and I tucked it away in my brain. I stepped back from my door as Agnes began closing it. Kaitlin stepped deeper into her room too, trying to hide the look of fear in her eyes. I nodded to her, as if to say, "It will be okay. We are safe here."

But I knew better. We were far from safe.

As my door closed, I stepped closer to its cross-shaped window and peered out across to Kaitlin. Her face filled her window as well. I glanced up at the marker over her door and studied it. Its familiarity poked at me, as if trying to remind me of something important. It held the numbers '235' and I wondered what their significance could be.

Then, as I dropped my eyes back to Kaitlin's, motion in the window of the door next to hers caught my attention. A face pressed against the window and stared across at me. She moved up and down as if bouncing from excitement. Then her voice burst through to us and filled the hallway. My heart skipped a beat and I jumped with happiness but at the same time I lifted my finger to my mouth to shush her.

But she still yelled for us.

"Finally! Jesus Christ!" she blasted. "What the hell did they do to you? You look like shit!"

Her voice echoed through the hall and I prayed Nurse Totten wasn't in earshot.

Kaitlin stared across at me in disbelief, waiting for a confirmation and without hesitation, I gave it to her.

I mouthed her name to Kaitlin.

"It's Emma!"

To read more, The Excited Ward is available on Amazon or check with your local library.

Made in United States
Troutdale, OR
09/20/2025